MURDER ON A PHILOSOPHICAL NOTE

(Blood on the Lake Path)

MURDER ON A PHILOSOPHICAL NOTE
(Blood on the Lake Path)

Shelley Glodowski

Copyright © 2006 by Shelley Glodowski

All rights reserved. No part of this book shall be reproduced or transmitted in any form or by any means, electronic, mechanical, magnetic, photographic including photocopying, recording or by any information storage and retrieval system, without prior written permission of the publisher. No patent liability is assumed with respect to the use of the information contained herein. Although every precaution has been taken in the preparation of this book, the publisher and author assume no responsibility for errors or omissions. Neither is any liability assumed for damages resulting from the use of the information contained herein.

This is a work of fiction. Names, characters, places, and incidents either are the product of the author's imagination or are used fictitiously. Any resemblance to actual events or locales or persons, living or dead, is entirely coincidental.

ISBN 0-7414-3193-9

Published by:

INFINITY
PUBLISHING.COM

1094 New DeHaven Street, Suite 100
West Conshohocken, PA 19428-2713
Info@buybooksontheweb.com
www.buybooksontheweb.com
Toll-free (877) BUY BOOK
Local Phone (610) 941-9999
Fax (610) 941-9959

Printed in the United States of America

Printed on Recycled Paper

Published June 2006

OTHER MYSTERIES BY SHELLEY GLODOWSKI:

MURDER ON THE WRONG NOTE:

"Shelley Glodowski's first book is a corker! Murder mystery, suspense filled thriller, and a romance all rolled into one. All in all it was a well written and enjoyable read that works on many levels. The author created a fine ensemble cast of characters and developed them nicely. I especially appreciated the decent, likeable good guys in this book. She writes well and spins a fine tale."

-Laurel Johnson for Midwest Book Review

"Write about what you know" is familiar advice for writers and Shelley Glodowski follows it to a T. She knows the world of rock and roll bands inside out. She's played with one for years. So, when she sets out to write a mystery, what better background could there be?"

-Lana Waite, Author (Saratoga, CA)

"Some might say it's coincidence, but when many years of someone's life are centered around these two strains of creativity, rock 'n' rolling and read 'n' writing, it's only natural that the two would flow together and, ultimately, mutually reinforce one another. In this case, the result is MURDER ON THE WRONG NOTE (2002), Glodowski's first novel, which is a combination of a rock 'n' roll tour and the "tour de force" of a murder investigation tangled in the bass-line of drugs, money, greed, and celebrity."

-Gregory Rutledge, Assistant Professor of English, University of Nebraska-Lincoln, NE

This book is dedicated to my husband, Randy, who is still the best rock 'n' roller of this or any other generation. It is also dedicated to my animals, whose tender love helped and hindered through times of intense concentration. I love you all! Keep on rockin'!!

I've always believed in the power of the mind to shape reality.
   -Shelley Glodowski

Rock on Gold Dust Woman...
   -Stevie Nicks

Acknowledgments

First of all, thanks to my darling husband who backs whatever hair brained scheme I come up with, including my writing.

Thanks to my "mystery consultant," the famous and infamous George Hesselberg, who plodded through my story and helped to correct it, shape it, and give me fresh ideas.

Thanks to my friends and proof readers Sioux Saloka, Jeanne Felix, Nancy Cox, Mary Steinbrecher (who also contributed countless ideas) and my husband Randy, whose quick eye found what I missed.

Thanks to the University of Wisconsin-Madison, which is filled with many kind and generous souls and is truly a wondrous place to visit and work. Thanks to Professor Rob Streiffer, who gave me lots of ideas and pointed me in the right direction. Thanks to Tasia Persson, who provided me with information.

Physical Plant and the campus police were, as always, most helpful in providing me with the campus ghost stories and a visit through the infamous campus tunnels, hosted by James Gibson.

I would also like to thank my counterpart at the University of Minnesota Department of Philosophy, Susan Wittel, for kindly e-mailing me a description of our sister department at the University of Minnesota.

Finally, I'd like to thank the Department of Philosophy, for all the helpful comments and support of my writing. You are truly the best!

Chapter 1

Dawn splashed up from the horizon like a French Impressionist painting; hues of rose, lavender, turquoise, and hyacinth twirling together in an exciting summer frolic. The sun beamed down on the moist earth with the promise of a glorious day. Birds chirped their approval of the proceedings as crystalline water from Lake Mendota lapped lazily against the shore. Green growth was everywhere.

Robert McIntyre's thoughts were miles away as his feet systematically pounded the path, setting up a one-two cadence. His athletic body pushed air in and out of his lungs in a rhythmic symbiosis with his limbs. He left his body on automatic pilot as his mind synthesized the beginning of a new day. He jogged three miles every morning, even in winter, and it was routine and exhilarating for him.

The lake path runs from Memorial Union at the University of Wisconsin in Madison to Picnic Point, known as a trysting place for young lovers in fast cars. The University sprawls all around the area, from Park Street, where the path begins, cob webbing in all directions, covering much of the inner city area with its majestic buildings named after long dead academics and entrepreneurs.

Lake Mendota laps against the shores of the University, granting many an office a spectacular, ever-changing panorama, mixed with the scent of algae in the late summer months. The University is secure in its reputation as a stunning place, and it is the first impression of many a visitor and delighted new hire. McIntyre held a full professor position in the Department of Bioethics, with an adjunct position in Philosophy. Philosophy happily paid a small percentage of his salary to be able to count him among their ranks.

Although his main love was research as a Biologist, he also held a PhD in Philosophy with a specialty in Ethics, making him an unusual scholar and highly marketable. As a graduate student, he had had the misfortune of witnessing abuses in the scientific field, and he had resolved to use his formidable intelligence and degrees for the good of mankind.

His research took off when questions began to arise in the media as Neo-cons tried to reshape the abortion argument. He was a popular lecturer, and his steady stream of articles help bolster the scientific point of view. This rare combination of talents made him much sought after by students seeking wisdom and rationale in their young worlds.

He had been at the University for ten happy years, long enough to climb the ranks of tenure from Assistant to Associate Professor in the first six years, with a full professorship following. McIntyre had flown through the process, ranking high in teaching evaluations and producing more than the necessary number of publications. It only took three years after that to gain promotion to full Professor, after a counter offer from another university threatened to snatch him from the halls of Wisconsin. The two departments sent desperate memos to sympathetic Deans, and enough money was scraped together to make a retention offer which McIntyre relished. He had made it, and he was doing something he loved.

Tall at six feet, with chestnut brown hair and chocolate brown eyes to match, McIntyre was dashing, but still retained the distracted look of the scholar intent upon his own research. He normally dressed in fashionable pants, with either casual sweaters or the latest in Lands End pullovers; creating the academic look which made female students swoon and feminine colleagues take a second look as he passed, unaware of the sensation he was causing.

McIntyre's wife, Janey, was a high school English teacher at one of the Madison high schools. Janey was blonde, five foot four, with pert shoulder length hair and a no-nonsense attitude. Their two daughters, Rhonda and Kirsten, were eight and ten years of age. They loved soccer, going to movies, and skiing. The family spent each Christmas at a ski resort, happily perfecting their downhill technique, although lately the girls had discovered skiboarding.

McIntyre was considering whether or not he would like to run for Chair of the Bioethics Department. Many of his faculty cohorts urged him to run, as he had an agreeable personality plus the backbone to make tough decisions. The position of Chair carried a considerable amount of power, particularly in regard to salaries and grants, and the history of the department was rife with examples of poor stewardship in the position. The disadvantage of taking on the position at this point in his career was that it would rob McIntyre of the energy and time he needed to pursue his own academic interests.

These and many other thoughts swirled through McIntyre's brain while the physiological effects of the jogging coursed through his body. He mentally organized his schedule for the day. There would be meetings with the University about his start-up company Bio-Xen. The name of the company was his own private joke...Bio for Biology and Xen for xenophobia, or the fear of something new.

The company's finances were at a critical juncture, and he needed to make a presentation to a group of prospective stockholders. The University had very strict protocols for research procedures, and McIntyre wanted to present himself in the very best light. The future of his company depended upon it.

Absorbed in his thoughts, McIntyre didn't notice that another set of feet had joined him on his run. The sun rose higher in the sky now, and perspiration was starting to bead on his forehead. His heart rate was up, and he could feel some strain in his thighs and calves. His knees had begun giving him more problems of late, and he wondered if he could keep up his accustomed exercise routine.

He became aware that the footsteps behind him seemed to match his own pace. Funny, he'd hardly ever run into fellow joggers at this time of the morning. He increased his speed a little out of a primitive urge to avoid confrontation. He felt uneasy, but didn't let himself dwell on the thought. He slowed a little to catch his breath. The footsteps sounded closer. *I wonder if this is what criminals feel like when they are chased,* McIntyre mused to himself, still not alarmed. After all, he was on campus, and he always had felt safe here before.

Suddenly feeling nervous, sweat began running down his armpits. He began to review what he could remember about a self-defense course taken long ago as an undergraduate. He chided himself for being paranoid. It was no doubt just another jogger.

He turned to see a heavily muscled man with short-cropped hair, a square jaw, and an unfriendly look. Something about him seemed familiar, but McIntyre couldn't quite see him, because the sun was now too bright. McIntyre began to panic. Was he going to be mugged? The jogger behind him didn't look as if he was out for a fun run.

McIntyre's brain went into high gear. What were his options? Not many. On one side was Lake Mendota, with a steep embankment leading down to the lake. On the other side was a hill which led up to the University buildings which occupied Observatory Drive: Social Sciences; and Liz Waters Hall, a women's dormitory.

As he desperately looked for an escape, the jogger suddenly grabbed him from behind, and all he felt was a searing pain as his throat was expertly slit. McIntyre sank down, as his body went into shock. He thought of his wife and daughters, seeing them reach out to him. Would his life insurance be enough to get them through? He thrashed, fighting his fate. This must be a mistake. Those were his last thoughts.

The jogger ran in place, watching the results of his work. He was sure taking a long time to die. Too much blood. He stayed and stared dispassionately until McIntyre stopped moving.

The murderer turned to run back the way he had come when he heard someone gasp. Uh oh, was that someone who could identify him? He heard someone call out. That was all he needed, someone upsetting his plans. He wouldn't allow that to happen.

He hid behind a bush to see who the intruder was. He couldn't afford to have any loose ends. His intake of breath indicated that there was indeed someone who was an uninvited guest. Her fate was sealed in that moment.

Chapter 2

Sam and Ian got lost looking for their new apartment located on East Johnson. East Johnson is one of the "main side streets" in Madison, knifing through the famed State Street sending a flurry of unforgiving traffic hurtling towards destinations either in the downtown section or on their way to the politically correct/working class East side of Madison. The East side traditionally housed some of the best blues and rock n' roll before the West side took notice, and took over with their own brand of clubs. East-side Johnny morphed into West-side Johnny.

"Why are these streets going in every which direction," Ian grumped, as Sam desperately tried to make sense of the Madison map.

"I don't think this town is laid out in a grid pattern," Sam commented, twisting a piece of her red hair around her finger. "Geez, what a screwy city...ah, there it is." She pointed to East Johnson, and Ian made a right turn off of Wisconsin Avenue. They had cruised around the downtown Square of Madison, a uni-directional racetrack that surrounded the historical Capitol building and velvety manicured lawns.

It was August 15th, or "moving day," as it is known in college towns. The streets were jammed with students, couches, trash, and traffic. It was chaos, but most people took it in stride. After all, this was the Mad City.

Sam was on a leave of absence from the Cleveland Police Department. Ian's band, *Heartthrob,* which starred had just finished their tour in support of their first CD, *"Under Cover."*

Ian played percussion in the band, which was actually a cover for his job as an FBI agent. Together, he and Sam had solved the mystery of who killed the booking agent, LeMar Ridley, in Cleveland, Ohio. In spite of the murder, the band survived and the tour was a smash.

The band was taking a much needed vacation, and Ian and Sam had decided that Madison was far enough away from Minneapolis, where *Heartthrob's* agency, *Phoenix Booking,* operated. Ridley had willed the agency to Patty Boyd, and Patty and her fiancé, Robert Pierce, now ran the agency and managed *Heartthrob.* A wedding was in the works, and the band was the featured entertainment.

Now it was time for Ian and Sam to set up their own household and explore their relationship. Sam planned on taking some law courses at the University of Wisconsin, with the option of enrolling full time.

They hoped the setup would be perfect for their new private investigation firm. Sam could further her own career, and Ian, who was also on leave from the FBI, would play with the band for the foreseeable future. Their savings and Ian's earnings from the tour would keep them solvent for the time being.

"Ah, here we are," Ian said, as he parked their van outside of a well kept Victorian house.

"It's beautiful." Sam clambered out of the van and stared critically at their new home. It was unfurnished, and they would have to wait for the movers to deliver their combined households of furniture and then try to make sense out of their possessions, but it felt good to be on solid ground again. The past few months had been filled with plane rides, hotels, searching for restaurants, and screaming fans in huge auditoriums.

"So, let's check out our new digs," Ian winked at Sam. They had already picked up their keys at the management company.

"All I want right now is a bathroom," Sam said, gritting her teeth. "Better see how the kitties are doing," Sam retrieved the two cabs in which two very pissed off cats were ensconced.

Cleo was Sam's white and black American Shorthair who had been her sole support during tough times in Cleveland. Sam had been surprised and delighted to discover that Ian had a gray tabby named Quincy, who was about Cleo's age. The two cats had, surprisingly, hit it off. But at the moment, they were expressing their displeasure by biting, caterwauling, and scratching.

"Shush! You're going to get us tossed out of town before we even step inside our new digs," Sam hissed at the uncooperative felines. She dug some treats out of her purse, and the clamor was replaced by chewing.

"Well, that shut them up for the time being," Sam pulled herself out of the back of their SUV, copper red hair falling forward into her brilliant blue eyes; her lanky five foot ten frame gracefully sliding out onto the sidewalk. She caught Ian watching her and blushed. His reddish-chestnut locks were stuffed under a navy baseball cap with a *Heartthrob* logo.

"What?" Sam demanded, catching the sparkle in his eyes and the grin on his face.

"You're such a great kitty mommy," Ian laughed. "You have more patience with the little monsters than I do."

"Well, let's get our stuff and the wee fiends inside before we cook to death." Sam handed Ian one of the cat cabs. "I want to call my cousin, Anni, to tell her we've arrived." Sam's cousin, Anni Cassidy, was the administrator in Philosophy at the University and had promised to come over and help with household setup and the details of getting the agency started.

The door to the house sported a new lock, and they had just stepped inside carrying a load from their van when Sam's cell phone rang. It was the moving company.

The next several hours were taken up with finding places for the furniture and the unending boxes. It was going to take a while to organize, even though they had already disposed of redundant furniture. But the walls were all painted a soft shade, and the house had terrific original woodwork.

Ian went to work setting up the stereo system, and Sam made sure boxes were placed in correct rooms. She shut the kitties in an upstairs bedroom so they wouldn't scamper out an open door.

By the end of the afternoon major pieces of furniture were in place and Sam had unpacked a few boxes in each room. Ian finished the stereo, and they both collapsed on the couch and released the cats from their prison.

"We still need to get groceries," Sam pointed out as she came in to check on Ian's progress.

"We'll find a place for dinner and then worry about stocking the 'frig." Ian said as he opened boxes containing his extensive CD collection. "Don't worry, it'll all come together."

"Groceries first, beer second, dinner later," Sam grunted, grabbing van keys and heading out the door.

Chapter 3

Anni Cassidy sat in her office at the Department of Philosophy, staring out the window which overlooked Lake Mendota, one of two lakes which make up the Madison Isthmus. She saw a flurry of sailboats running around in small circles as a Hoofer's sailing coach yelled instructions.

Anni was in her mid-thirties, and had worked at the University for ten years. She was five foot six and blonde. Her blue/gray eyes could spit fire when she was crossed, but she was a wizard at keeping everything and everyone in the department on track. They valued her services, and she loved working with the Philosophy faculty.

Anni couldn't believe that Rob had been found dead on the lake path. A hysterical female jogger from the Biology department had found his prone body, and had dialed 911 to summon campus police.

Anni's boss and chair of the department, Bruce Wilkins, sat in her office, also in shock. "We just had dinner with Rob and his wife, Janey, last week," Bruce said sadly. "You just never think that something like this will happen to someone you know."

"Have you heard when the Memorial Service will be?" Anni asked Bruce gently.

Bruce looked at her fondly. "No, I don't know yet. But thanks for your concern, Anni. The Department appreciates your efforts. I'm just paralyzed by this atrocity. The police are coming over this morning to question some of the faculty members. Do you think we could have a murderer in the department? It could do us great harm on more levels than I care to think about at the moment."

Anni's clear blue eyes surveyed her distraught boss. She couldn't wrap her mind around the word "murder." She thought of the faculty. "It couldn't have been any of our group. Philosophers just don't strike me as the murdering type. Maybe it was just one of those random violent/rage murders. Has anyone escaped from the area prisons?"

"I don't know, and I really don't want to talk about it anymore. Say, don't you have a cousin who is setting up a new private detective firm coming to town? It's kind of a coincidence. Maybe she could help us."

"Well, you can certainly meet Sam and her boyfriend, Ian, if you'd like. Sam was a homicide detective in Cleveland, and Ian worked with the FBI," Anni answered, not certain if her boss was just making conversation. Still, it was a thought. She needed to give Sam and Ian a call to see if they'd arrived yet from Minneapolis, but another thought popped up.

"Why don't you call Janey to find out what time the service will be held? You could mention that my cousin is here and see if she is interested in hiring her."

"Good idea, I'll make the call and get back to you in a few minutes," Bruce said, clearly relieved at having a job that helped regain the feeling of control.

Janey was surprised that someone in Anni's position would have a cousin "in the detection business" as she put it, but she was more than happy for the suggestion.

"I'll do anything to find the person who did this," she told Bruce. "My children are in shock, and right now I'm pissed off. I'd like to..." she didn't think the sentence needed completion.

"I'm not making any promises, but I'll ask Anni to call her cousin. We'll have her and her partner at the memorial service to talk to you," Bruce replied.

Anni received the instructions with a somber expression, but she had every confidence that if anyone could uncover this murder, Sam could. She dug out her address book from her purse to look up Sam's cell phone number, with an eye to the clock to make sure she wasn't calling too early. It was 9:30 a.m., and she thought she would be safe.

"Hello?" Sam's voice sounded a little foggy with sleep. She had just gotten up when the phone rang.

"Sam! You're here!" Anni whooped. Sam and Ian had just rolled out of bed, having stayed up late the night before. Sam had discovered State Street and East Towne, and had hit both places in a shopping frenzy.

"Anni! It's so great to hear your voice," Sam said, instantly awake. Anni was one of her favorite people in the world. Sam had always looked up to her cousin as she was growing up. "We spent the entire day moving in. I'm so stiff I can hardly move! We didn't go to bed until 2:00 a.m."

Anni made appropriate clucking sounds of sympathy and more small talk before getting to the purpose of her call.

"Listen, Sam," Anni began, turning serious. "One of our faculty members was found murdered on the lake path just outside of our building. My boss, Bruce, talked with his wife, Janey, and she is wondering if you would look into it."

"A murder! I didn't think Madison was large enough to have murders." Sam hesitated for a second, thinking furiously. "Of course, we would be glad to help. Luckily we took care of the licensing, bonding, and insurance for the detective agency before we got here. We didn't think that we'd get business this fast. I'm so sorry to hear it was one of your faculty members. You must be devastated."

"It's pretty tense around here," Anni agreed. "Incidentally, the memorial service is tomorrow. I'm sure you have things to do to get organized today. Could you come to the service? I'll introduce you to Janey, Rob's wife."

"Is this Janey's idea?" Sam asked. "We don't want to get involved unless she specifically asks for us."

"Well, it was Bruce's idea, my boss. He talked with Janey, and she agreed that she wanted someone besides the police to look into this. She thought that it might be easier to find the murderer."

"What time and place?"

"It's at St. Paul's Chapel right on the University campus. Just take Gorham Street, which runs parallel to Johnson, your street. Turn right at Langdon, then left on Lake Street. There's a ramp right there you can park in. The service is at 3:00 p.m."

Ian finished his shower and came into the room just as Sam was finishing her conversation with Anni.

"What's up?" Ian asked Sam, catching her expression. He was beginning to see the patterns. "It's another murder, isn't it? We don't even have our boxes unpacked!"

Sam nodded. "I guess murder just follows me around." She gave Ian a peck on the cheek. "I guess that's part of my karma."

"I wonder if I was busy following you around in another life solving mysteries," Ian said as he headed off for a morning shower. Sam stuck her tongue out at his retreating figure.

Chapter 4

Sam and Ian had no trouble finding their way to the St. Paul Center on campus. "Just go to the end of State Street," everyone told them when they asked for directions.

"I think I'm getting the hang of this place," Ian commented, as he drove the van into the parking ramp, "Mad City, indeed."

Sam laughed, and then turned serious. "Another murder, I was hoping we could start the agency with small things...you know...affairs, collections, that sort of thing. I wonder if this is going to be the story of our lives."

Ian looked at her affectionately. "I can handle it if you can. You're the one who is trying to go back to school. It'll all work out, you'll see."

Ian and Sam signed in and entered the center. They easily spotted the widow and her two children. They looked stoic, but their heartbreak was apparent. The two girls, carbon copies of their mother, cried and looked bewildered. Janey gently comforted them, and they clung to her in grief.

"Doesn't look like a domestic murder," Ian commented to Sam, who nodded soberly.

Janey McIntyre found Sam and Ian after the service. She carried herself with quiet dignity, and her daughters emulated her style. "I'm Janey McIntyre. I'm pleased to meet you, although I wish the circumstances were different. You're just as Anni described you. We're very fond of our Anni."

"It's nice to meet you, Mrs. McIntyre." Sam and then Ian shook her hand solemnly. "We're very sorry for your loss and hope we can be of some assistance."

Janey gave them a wan smile. "The police have been very helpful so far. But I wanted some very personal effort to be put into this crime. I'm now determined to see my husband's killer brought to justice." Her eyes filled with tears. She shook her head to compose herself and straightened her shoulders and gave them an apologetic smile.

"Other than my daughters, this is now my mission in life." Her eyes flashed for a moment.

"Perhaps you could stop over at our office, say tomorrow morning?" Ian suggested. "We would like to ask you some questions before we accept the case. We want to ensure that we *can* add something to the police investigation."

"I'm sure the police are doing all they can," Janey said, wiping her eyes with a tissue. "But many murders are never solved. I don't even know if I'm in danger, or my daughters. If something happened to them…"

"We'll be happy to talk to you tomorrow, Mrs. McIntyre," Sam said sympathetically. "We think the world of Anni and would do anything to help her or anyone who is a friend of hers."

"Thanks. This is just so confusing. I look forward to talking to you, say at 10:00?"

Sam pulled out a business card with their new address, a product of their scurrying around the day before and inwardly breathed a sigh of relief that they could present themselves in a professional manner.

This was a new town, a new life for her and Ian. And they had their first case.

"By the way," Janey said, almost as an afterthought. "This could get very complicated. My husband was just setting up a new company. I don't understand everything he was doing, but there are a lot of crazy people who might object to research with cloning, and I think they dealt with it in some way or another."

Sam was instantly alert. "Does he have any notes, or something written up that describes his new company?"

"I'll look at his desk to see if there are any papers to bring to the interview tomorrow," Janey said, retreating into herself again, as she dabbed at her eyes. "That is, if I can find something relevant. He was methodical, but his desk was always a mess."

They all laughed. "Just bring whatever catches your eye and let us handle it," Ian suggested.

"The police have already been through the house, so I think that would be all right," Janey agreed.

"So we'll see you at ten then?" Sam asked gently, making eye contact with Janey.

Janey sighed. "That would be fine. I know exactly how to find your house. I'll be there."

"We've just moved in, so please pardon our clutter," Sam said, and Janey rewarded her with a small smile.

Chapter 5

Sam woke and showered the next morning to the smell of bacon and eggs. She followed her nose and wandered into the kitchen.

"A rock star, an FBI agent, and you cook too?" She gave Ian a peck on the cheek.

"I used to be a short-order cook in college, and I found out I really enjoyed it. So I began to experiment, and I became a half-way decent chef. This is child's play," he shrugged. Their relationship was still very new, and other than the obvious physical attraction, they were finding more similarities than differences. Sam wasn't a bad cook herself, but she tended to enjoy making salads and chocolate desserts. Ian was strictly a meat and potatoes kind of guy.

Sam cocked an eyebrow. "Well, let the games begin, a point for the big guy with all the red hair," Sam laughed at Ian's expression. Ian, hair tousled, stood before the stove whipping up a scrambled eggs and shrimp concoction.

"I'm surprised you found the frying pans," Sam commented, sniffing the air appreciatively.

"Number three box in the kitchen set," Ian mumbled, intent on the egg dish. "Would you handle the liquid part of the meal?"

Sam hastily opened boxes looking for a pitcher for orange juice. She emitted a grunt that sounded something like "all right" as she located the plastic container. She found a manual can opener, since the electric one was buried somewhere, and started cranking the tin open when the phone rang, which had just been hooked up the afternoon before.

17

"Sam! It's Anni. Hope I'm not interrupting anything?" Anni chuckled into the phone. "Do you want me to come over and help set things up before your interview with Janey? I thought you might need some help."

"We're just making breakfast. How soon can you get here?" Sam looked at Ian meaningfully, and he threw a couple more eggs in the mix.

"Ten minutes. And don't worry about me seeing a mess. That's why I'm coming...to get you organized. Is your computer set up yet?"

"I see your point," Sam said. "Come on over. Do you need directions?"

Anni just giggled. "I was born here...remember? I can find any street in this town."

Anni rang their doorbell a short while later. Sam and Ian had dashed for the bedroom to throw on some clothes and were just putting the food on the table when Anni walked in.

"First things first," Sam indicated a chair for Anni to sit down and get started on her meal. "I have a feeling it's going to be a long day, so we need to fortify ourselves."

"Tell us more about Janey," Ian suggested, as he sat down and put a paper towel on his lap. They had forgotten to buy napkins during their storm of the grocery store the day before.

"Do you mean, do I think that Janey could kill her husband? No way," Anni shook her head emphatically. "They seemed like a very committed couple."

"No affairs, then? No gossip?" Sam asked.

"Well, the department has the obvious affairs you would expect from a group of people working together," Anni answered. "You might want to hear about some of those later, after you interview Janey. She might even be able to supply some information. Philosophers tend to like to socialize, and I'm sure things get noticed."

"Another line of questioning," Ian commented.

They cleared dishes into the dishwasher and Anni went into their study to set up the computer. They had agreed that she would take notes of the interview with Janey, since Anni was familiar with her. It took Anni and Sam a half an hour to pull the computer components out of the box and connect cables. The monitor is always the heaviest, so Ian hoisted it on to the computer desk.

Just as they had turned on the computer for the first time in its new home, the doorbell rang. Janey McIntyre stood on the step with an uncertain smile on her face.

"Hi Janey," Sam took her elbow. "There are still boxes we haven't unpacked, so excuse the mess."

Janey looked around at the neatly stacked boxes and smiled. "This is actually neater than some spaces in my house, especially Robert's study." A cloud passed over her face and her eyes went dull as she felt a stab of loneliness.

"Sorry, the wounds are still new. I just can't believe he's gone. I keep expecting him to walk through the door at home. Our dog, Fife, is heartbroken. So am I."

"Make yourself comfortable. Would you like some coffee?" Sam asked, giving Janey what she hoped was a reassuring smile. It was time to begin probing for answers.

Chapter 6

Janey McIntyre stepped from the warm morning sunshine into front foyer. Sam led her into a spacious living room and she admired the natural oak woodwork, which had been routed by hand more than seventy-five years before. The walls were a pleasant shade of sand, and the furniture Sam and Ian had moved in was soft and comfortable looking.

Janey gratefully accepted a cup of coffee and a leftover muffin, since she hadn't eaten anything yet that morning. Her stomach was still jittery from the shock of her husband's death, and she'd lost her appetite. The bite of muffin stuck in her throat.

"I'm sorry," she apologized, digging in her purse for a tissue. "I just can't seem to wrap my mind around what's happened here. I got up this morning looking for Rob, until I remembered that he's gone." She blew her nose into the tissue and rapidly blinked her eyes, trying to regain her composure.

Ian and Sam nodded sympathetically. Anni walked over and put her arms around Janey and gave her a hug. Janey clung to Anni for a moment. Then Anni gave her a pat on the back and silently resumed her place at the computer.

"Is it all right if Anni stays for the interview? She is going to type some notes for us so we'll have a record of the interview. Sam will also make notes into her laptop, if that is all right with you." Janey nodded her assent.

"Okay, let's begin," Sam said in her practiced detective voice. "I want you to tell us what happened, as nearly as you can remember."

"Well, Rob went out for his morning jog. He was a very routine-oriented person, except for his desk. Someone snuck up behind him just as he was at the mid-point of the trail that runs along the lake. Another jogger, a Marie Cavendish, found him I think. His throat had been cut, and apparently he bled to death." She clenched her fingers.

"Where were you at the time of the murder?" Sam asked after a few seconds.

"I was at Memorial High School, preparing my lesson plans for the day. I teach English," Janey answered. "Both of the girls were also at school. They called me to say there had been an accident with Rob. But I thought it might be a car accident. I never imagined that someone would want to hurt him. He was such a good man."

"What have the police told you so far?" Ian asked, while Sam tapped on her computer. The sounds of Anni's fingers clicking on the keyboard on the other side of the room could also be heard.

"The police have questioned people in all the buildings that run along the lake path. But it's like trying to find a needle in a haystack. The University community contains thousands of people."

"Is there anyone you might suspect?" Ian pressed on.

Janey's eyes grew large. "That is a very difficult question," she hedged. "If you mean, were there people who Rob didn't like, the answer is obviously yes. Was there anyone who would commit murder? I have no idea."

"Tell us a little about both of the departments," Sam urged her gently. "Who were the difficult personalities?"

Janey looked over at Anni for support. Anni gravely nodded her head at Janey, urging her on.

"Well, there were about eight or ten people who would be considered 'the power elite' in Philosophy. You know...the big salaried people; people who consistently scored the biggest grants; people who wrote the most books and articles. Academics is a very competitive business. It is probably the only arena, besides sports, where the individual is actually rewarded for out-maneuvering their adversaries."

"How about the Bioethics Department," Ian asked, his blue eyes sympathetic.

"Well, the hard sciences have a different face entirely than Philosophy," Janey screwed up her face in thought. "Scientists tend to be less sociable. Some don't even pay attention to personal grooming. But they surprise you, because they might be the most brilliant people of all."

"Could you jot down some notes on individuals to give to us?" Sam asked.

Janey's face turned ashen at the request. "I...I guess so. You mean you want me to list everything I know about each person?"

"That would be most helpful," Ian nodded sagely. "And, get it to us as soon as possible, if you can manage it. We know you have enough on your mind, but any information you could give us would be most helpful."

Janey nodded, eyebrows knit together in a frown. "Whatever it takes," she said softly. "This is my life now."

"Is there anyone staying with you? Or at least watching your house, until this situation is resolved?" Sam asked. Ian nodded to Sam, both of them thinking the same thing. She would need protection.

Anni spoke up at that point. "I have a really good friend in the Madison Police Department. He is a detective. He used to work on campus as a policeman. He might know of someone who could help."

Janey nodded in agreement. "I would feel better if someone was watching our house for the next couple of weeks."

"Did you find anything about your husband's new company that you could share with us?" Sam asked, remembering the conversation at the memorial service.

Janey shrugged. "I didn't find anything that jumped out at me. It's so technical that I don't understand most of what the company is doing. But I do know that they were planning on investigating new cures for diabetes. Maybe that would ruffle a few feathers."

"We'll look into that further," Sam promised.

Janey opened her purse. "Here is $5,000 cash to get you started," she said. "If you could find someone who could watch our house, I would be most grateful. I'm scared stiff, and I don't want my girls to be in danger."

"Okay, this is a down payment," Ian said. "We charge $300.00 per day, plus expenses. We'll keep a running tally and bill you when your account is depleted. Is that satisfactory?"

"Just catch my husband's murderer," Janey said, straightening her spine. "That's your job."

"We'll do our best," Sam said. "What we need for you to jot down would be a rundown of the people in both departments; any professional jealousies; any affairs that you know about; any incidents of cheating or sabotage; what kind of parties; any drugs taken by anyone; anyone who would have something to gain by your husband's death."

* * * * *

Janey left, still dabbing her eyes. After they shut the door, Sam and Ian fixed their eyes on Anni.

"What," Anni eyed Sam suspiciously.

"Now it's your turn…" Sam said, nodding her head towards the couch. "…for the third degree."

Anni obligingly sat down on the couch, enjoying the feeling of the late-morning sun streaming on to her shoulders. She gave Sam and Ian a half smile, folded her arms and said "What?" She then unfolded her arms, to assure them that she wasn't hiding anything, and leaned in, ready for the inquisition.

"My, my, you are full of surprises," Sam began, chuckling. "I think you know someone who is helpful in just about any emergency." Anni's smirk gave her away.

"Well, I'm building manager," Anni began in her defense. They all laughed. "Okay. Now what dirt do you want to know about?"

"Who would you suspect?" Ian asked the benchmark question. "Try to connect the dots…or personalities."

Anni stared at him for a minute. She got up and walked around, scratching her head. Finally, she turned to them.

"I think it has something to do with his company, or it might be professional jealousy," Anni offered. "There are some characters in our department, to be sure. There is Fred Canon, who likes to collect antique weapons. He might just be weird enough to do it."

Sam flipped open her laptop again and began to tap keys. She typed the word **"Suspects"** at the top of the page. "Okay, who is he and why would he do it?"

"Well, he teaches Ethics. When Rob came in, he was competition, if you know what I mean. He's definitely an oddball, in an intellectual way. I haven't seen it, but I've heard he has an entire basement full of antique weapons. He's abnormally shy. Doesn't that fit some kind of profile?"

"Is there anyone else?" Ian asked.

"Well, there is one couple that seems to cause a lot of problems around here," Anni went on. "Maybe Rob caught them at something. They are pretty nasty people; I wouldn't be surprised if they were into drugs either. They act pretty weird at times. Their names are Phyllis Litchfield and Tom Jacobs."

"Sounds lovely," Sam commented, as she typed.

"Don't get me started," Anni said, laughing.

"I see, and is there a nepotism policy? I assume the University of Wisconsin has such rules in place?" Ian asked, cocking an eyebrow.

"Oh, yes. There is a written policy. But there is nothing against faculty being married, as long as one does not supervise the other. I've heard of some cases where the rules were bent to allow a variation." Anni's voice trailed off. She didn't want to say too much.

"Well, enough. I've got some errands to do and you two need to plot strategy...or whatever it is you detectives/cops do. Just give me a call when you need me again. I'm happy to help in any way I can. It's fun doing something that has nothing to do with academics for a change. But for now, I'm bushed. See ya later." Anni gave a cheery wave as she headed for the door.

"Oh, Ian, it's been a pleasure. Welcome to the fold!" Anni called out as she strode through the threshold and out into the sunny fall day whose warmth mocked their somber activities.

Chapter 7

"So, we have to deal with a university bureaucracy and the attending politics," Ian pulled at the back of his hair as he considered the implications of what Anni and Janey had said. "Sounds like a challenge," he commented wryly.

"Not only that, but we have to sort through not only faculty and staff, but their areas of expertise," Sam replied, staring at Ian as she talked. That was her way of organizing her thoughts, and Ian was getting used to that bright-eyed look.

"But first we need to make contact with the Madison Police Department. We want them on our side. No telling when we might need some *undercover equipment*, Sam joked, referring to their first case together, when she had attended one of *Heartthrob's* concerts decked out in the finest listening gear the St. Paul Police department could provide. It had been an experience.

Ian cracked up, remembering. "Well, hopefully we won't have to worry about listening devices at any of our future concerts." His smile vanished, and he was all business again. "So, what's our next step, Red?"

Sam grinned back. Ian had picked up the nickname that her old boss, Jerry Malone, used for her. "Seems like we've made a lot of changes lately, huh Dude?"

"Yeah, a lot of changes," Ian said softly. "But for now, I'm feeling in need of a nap. Anyone care to join me?"

"You don't have to ask twice," Sam made a dash for the bedroom, with Ian in hot pursuit. He kicked the door shut and took her in his arms. "I've wanted to do this all day."

"So, which angle should we tackle first?" Sam asked Ian later. She propped herself up on to the pillow and nudged Ian until his eyes fluttered open.

"Huh?" Ian asked, still sleepy from their lovemaking. He emitted a huge yawn, which turned into a groan. "What are you talking about?" He crinkled his brilliant blue eyes at her and furrowed his brows.

"We still have the entire afternoon! We have to get going. There's time to check out the murder scene. Come on, get up and let's go!" Sam scrambled out of bed, and Ian reluctantly stumbled after her. They pushed the cats off the covers and threw clothes on. The cats expressed silent displeasure, backs turned and tails swishing. The bedroom door was then shut as they dressed, which caused demanding meows on the other side of the door.

"Maybe they need a nice puppy to keep them in line," Ian joked. "Do we know how to get there?"

"Of course I do! The campus is at the end of State Street, and the lake is to the right. How hard can it be to find? Besides, I've got my cell phone, so we can always call Anni if we get lost. I'll call Detective Joel Drake, Anni's friend." Sam walked into the living room searching for a phone book.

Forty-five minutes later Sam and Ian arrived at the scene of the crime. Yellow police tape blocked off the crime scene. The ground was still stained with blood, which formed a grisly contrast to the serenity of the lake path. They waited for another ten minutes for Detective Drake's appearance. Finally he appeared, his warm grin lighting up a confident face full of intelligence.

"You must be Sam and Ian. Anni is excited you're here. She's all alone, so I'm glad she finally has relations in the vicinity. You never know when you're going to need some help."

Detective Drake was a former linebacker with the Wisconsin Badger football team, which is how Anni met him. He was a star in his day, and appeared one day in the Philosophy Department, looking to fulfill his academic Communications writing requirement.

Anni looked up to see her favorite football star, excitedly asked him for his autograph, and a grand friendship ensued. Detective Joel Drake acted as the Madison Police Department's liaison with the University of Wisconsin, so about once every two months he and Anni had lunch together. They shared a love of sports, and Anni had even become godmother to Joel's two kids.

"We've heard a lot about the great Joel Drake," Ian grinned, offering his hand. "We're big fans, so this is indeed a privilege." His face crinkled with pleasure.

Joel blushed incongruously. "Same here," he said. He had heard all about *Heartthrob* and Ian and Sam's exploits with the band. "I'm also a fan, so I guess we're off to a good start. So, how can I help you today?"

"Just by answering some questions," Sam began. "We don't want to step on any jurisdictional toes here. Mrs. McIntyre has hired us as private investigators to look into Professor McIntyre's death. Maybe we can help each other."

Joel gave a tight smile. "I'll give you what we've got, but I don't have much time. I have two other cases to investigate and three reports sitting on my desk. But you may want to talk with the deputy coroner. If I were you, that's where I'd start, after you look over the scene here."

"Can you tell me how the system works here? I know it's done in accordance to statute," Sam asked.

Joel flashed a grin. "That's true. In Wisconsin communities with less than five hundred thousand elect coroners to investigate death scenes to determine the cause of death, establish identity, and notify next of kin. They also obtain personal data and provide expert testimony in court.

They assist at autopsies, taking photographs and document evidence."

"Where was the autopsy performed?"

"At University Hospital," Joel answered. "Our medical examiner can also act as coroner if the coroner is on vacation or is sick. In this case, the coroner performed the autopsy."

"What was the time of death?" Sam asked. "What do you know about the details?"

"The subject's throat was slit from behind. Splatter marks indicate that someone came up, pulled his head back and slit the throat. He bled out on the ground. He couldn't have called out for help. We haven't gotten all the lab results back yet. But the time of death seems to have been about 7:15 a.m. He must have been an early bird." He shrugged. "Another jogger found him. You might want to talk to her. Her name is Marie Cavendish."

"Are there any suspects?"

He shrugged again. "It's too early to tell."

"Did they lift any footprints?" Ian asked.

"The ground was too hard to get a good imprint. It's been awfully dry around here lately."

"How about residue from the fingers of the victim; was there tissue under his fingernails that could be matched through DNA?"

"You have some good questions. You should start with the Coroner. I could try to get you an appointment with him. His name is Dave Kane." He looked at his watch. "He can probably tell you a lot more. Now I've got to scoot. You know…places to go, reports to write. Let me know if I can be of further help. I'm glad you are here to help. It was great meeting the two of you. Anni is a good friend."

"Well, it's a start," Ian said after Joel left. "But I guess we're stomping on his professional territory. He could have been a lot more standoffish. At least we have a contact in the police department, which could be very useful."

"I want to take a look around," Sam said, beginning to walk around the lake path area. "Maybe they missed something, although the indent team is usually thorough." She surveyed the area, scanning from side to side, trying to get a feel for the scene.

Ian shrugged and began his own search, but didn't find anything. Except for the blood and the yellow tape, it looked like an idyllic place.

Thinking something looked out of place, Sam walked over to a small tree and found a piece of black fabric. It blended in to the bark so perfectly that she could see how someone could miss it. She always carried plastic bags in her purse and pulled one out, careful not to touch the fabric with her fingers.

"It might be nothing, but maybe we have a bargaining chip. I'm sure the police are probably not too thrilled to have us mucking up their investigation."

Chapter 8

Sam and Ian wandered into the Madison Police Headquarters, located at 211 South Carroll. The Carroll Street station covered the Central District, encompassing the central area of the City of Madison.

The Department works closely with the University on such problems as the homeless who inhabit State Street, many of whom have serious substance abuse problems and occasionally roam into the halls of University buildings for warmth or theft.

"Okay, this is going to be a little weird," Sam commented.

"Oh, you'll win them over," Ian said. "Just remember what you did in Minneapolis." Sam had charmed some hard-boiled police who had a recalcitrant attitude towards her crime-solving abilities until she sorted through a difficult case that involved gang members and drugs.

Detective Drake looked up from his report as Sam and Ian walked in. "I didn't think I would see you two so soon," he commented in a neutral tone.

Sam dropped the plastic bag on his desk. "I'll trade you," she said, trying to keep a grin off of her face.

Drake looked surprised, and then gingerly took the bag from her. "Is this what I think it is?" He looked closely at the bag and shook his head. "I can't believe we missed this. But I guess anything's possible." He looked a little upset.

"I'm not trying to embarrass you or anything. But as soon as I found this, I thought it might be important." Sam gave him a tentative smile and gave him time to look at the small piece of black cloth she had found hanging on a branch.

Drake put the evidence bag on his desk and thought for a moment before answering. "I guess that reputation I've heard about is well deserved. Now, I suppose you would like me to set up an appointment for you with the deputy coroner." He shot a challenging look at Sam.

"Great!" Sam smiled. "One more question. Janey McIntyre is going to need some protection. Do you have any officers who would like to do some moonlighting?"

Joel scratched his short Afro. "I think we can accommodate you on that...there are always guys who want more hours. You are paying, of course?"

Sam and Ian nodded, trying to keep from grinning at each other. They were off to a good start.

"Oh, by the way," Joel told them. "You might want to interview the woman who found the body. Her name is Marie Cavendish. But I don't want you stepping on any toes, so be careful how you approach her. And, now, it's time for me to get back to work."

"Yes, I wrote down her name when you told us about her earlier. We'll be sure to follow up."

Sam heaved a sigh of relief after they left Joel's office. "Maybe we've made a new friend," she commented to Ian as they stepped out into the sunshine.

"Time will tell," Ian said shortly. "But now we have a lot of work to do. Our next step is the Coroner, don't you think, unless that beautiful head of yours has other ideas."

Sam looked at Ian thoughtfully. "No other ideas for now. The Coroner sounds like as good a next step as any. After that we'll hit the two departments, and we also need to find Marie Cavendish. She might have seen more than just finding the body. Lead on, Sherlock."

They placed a cell phone call to the Coroner's office who referred them to Dr. David Kane. They learned that the autopsy of Professor McIntyre had already been performed at the Pathology Department in the University of Wisconsin Hospital facility. But Dr. Kane would be happy to speak with them after he had received a phone call from Joel Drake.

"At least we're having the way paved for us," Sam said with a sigh of relief after she snapped shut her cell phone.

"Yeah, but if I know the police, we'll have to tread lightly," Ian told Sam. "They probably don't care that you were a hotshot detective."

Chapter 9

Dave Kane greeted Sam and Ian with a perfunctory nod as they were shown into his office at the Coroner's Department in the Public Safety Building on West Doty Street.

Dave Kane had held his position as Deputy Coroner for Dane County for about ten years. He was a product of the Madison Area Technical College with an associate degree in police science and medical technology. He was forty-three years of age, and had prematurely gray hair with a round bald spot. His round wire-rimmed glasses gave him a scholarly air. He stood at only 5'8" inches of height, and had to peer through his bifocals up at Ian and Sam.

"How can I help you today?"

"We are private investigators hired by Mrs. Janey McIntyre. Her husband, Robert McIntyre, was recently found murdered on the Lake Path at the University of Wisconsin."

"Oh yes…a very sad case. Professor McIntyre was attacked from behind. The murderer severed his carotid artery. It was an obvious homicide. It breaks the heart when one sees victims who are too young to die."

"Do you know from the cut if the murderer was left or right-handed?" Sam asked.

"Oh, he was definitely left-handed; accordingly the entry wound was on the right side of Professor McIntyre's neck." He emphasized his point by jabbing his neck.

"Have the lab tests come back yet? Were there any illegal drugs in his system, for instance steroids?"

"No illegal drugs. He had had a good breakfast before his run...cereal and orange juice. There was nothing to indicate that he was given or had taken any drugs prior to his murder."

"How about the cut itself, was it exceptionally deep?" Ian asked.

"The photographs of the deceased show the depth of the cut very clearly. His body has already been released to the family for burial, so we can't show it to you in person," Kane smiled at his own gallows humor.

"Can you give us some idea of whether this would have been a crime of passion, a hit, or a premeditated crime by some person with knowledge of knives?"

Kane scratched his bald spot absentmindedly. "I've never seen anything like this before. It's almost like the "Jack the Ripper" tales. Whoever killed this man used a surgical knife with a curved edge. I would say that it was a premeditated murder performed by a ruthless killer. The cut was very efficient; not too deep and not too shallow. This person knew what he was doing. He may even have had some military training."

"Could we see a copy of the photographs and autopsy report?" Sam asked.

"I'll have to clear it with the police department. Can I have my secretary fax it to you? It might take a day or so, but I think we could oblige. We want to see this case cleared up as quickly as possible, especially since it happened on University grounds. Parents get very agitated when they think there is a murderer loose at the University. I'm sure that your help will be appreciated by all concerned."

"We are grateful for any information you can give us. We'll do our best to help out with this case. If you can think of anything, please take this card with our phone number on it. I also have a cell phone," Sam said, as she pulled a card out of her purse. She smiled at Kane, impressed with his efficiency and willingness to share information.

Sam and Ian stepped back outside, enjoying the sunshine after breathing the re-circulated air of the building.

"I guess our next move is to visit the two departments," Sam said, giving voice to her thoughts. "Why don't we find some food first? I'm starved! Where can we eat?" Ian looked at her indulgently…she was always hungry after a particularly difficult interview.

"I noticed some restaurants on State Street. We could pick one out and have lunch there. Then we could walk over to see Anni in the Department of Philosophy. It's just about noon," Ian said, consulting his watch.

Lunch turned out to be gyros sandwiches from a Greek restaurant gracing State Street. As they ate, Sam typed in notes of their conversation with Dr. Kane into her now ever-present laptop.

"So we have a left-handed Jack the Ripper," Ian mused. "I sure hope that this individual is not a serial killer." Sam's head popped up with his last comment.

"It would certainly make our first month in Madison difficult if it is. The method does bother me though. I wonder if we could be dealing with someone who is in the medical profession. This is a large university town with a renowned medical school." She took another bite of her sandwich thoughtfully.

"I wonder how much experience they've had with a serial killer in this town, if any," Ian went on. He had taken the last bite of his sandwich and finished the beer he had sitting in front of him.

"I can't imagine they've had any," Sam said. "I don't remember anything in the literature, but these days one can never tell. We'll know more when we receive that autopsy report. So, what's next on the list?"

"I think we need to visit both departments, get a feel for the personnel involved. I'm not real fond of academic types, so I hope you can do most of the talking." He gave Sam a hard look. "I've had some bad experiences with those people."

Sam matched his look. "Okay, let me guess. Perhaps you got a bad grade in a required course? Or there was a professor who wasn't there for office hours? Or are you just afraid of highly intelligent people who live in the Ivory Tower?" She gave Ian a wicked grin.

Ian grunted, but didn't answer at first. A frown appeared on his forehead, as he remembered a bad experience. "I had a run-in with a professor once. I had written a paper for criminal justice, and his theories didn't fit in with my findings. So I got a 'B' in the course, when it should have been an 'A'." He pulled back one side of his mouth. "I guess you could call it the caprice of education."

"Indeed," Sam agreed. "I had a few bad experiences myself. But we mustn't let that interfere with our investigation. We're on the other side of the fence now, and we are evaluating the evaluators."

"Let's not forget Marie Cavendish. She found the body and if we question her, she may remember something she forgot to tell the police," Ian reminded Sam.

"She'll be next on the list after we visit the departments," Sam said.

They paid their bill, left a tip, and stepped out into another glorious late summer day. Wispy clouds skittered past a golden sun, reminding Sam of Arizona in the spring.

Chapter 10

Sam and Ian entered the boxy structure that served as Helen C. White Hall. Built after the tumultuous sixties, the all cement frame was meant to be a fortress against the possible rampages of drug-crazed hippies. Nestled into the tower is College Library, a more sensible structure. A walkway floats above College Library off of the third floor of Helen C. White, forming a merging of the two buildings. Underneath lie two layers of parking, which house vehicles at one of the "premium" parking lots on campus.

After what seemed an interminable wait for the two elevators, Sam pushed the button for fifth floor, and they emerged from the crush of students jostling for a spot. A short walk to the left and around the corner found them in Room 5185, the main office of the Philosophy Department.

Anni emerged from her office, grinning from ear to ear. "It is such fun to have family in the workplace; especially esteemed relatives," she beamed. Sam blushed, but looked pleased at the praise. Ian looked around at the startled staff, who whispered behind their hands. They were not used to seeing such a Herculean man in their environment. Curious eyes and whispering leaked out from the offices off of the main suite.

"Please, come in," Anni steered them into her office and shut the door with a sigh. "Pardon the snickers, but you have to understand that people with your, eh...physical presence...don't usually grace our department."

Ian blushed at this compliment and changed the subject. "We'd like to take a look around and talk with your staff and some of the faculty, if they are around." He looked around doubtfully. "I remember that faculty doesn't exactly keep nine-to-five hours from my days as an undergrad."

Sam shot Ian a warning look and got down to business. "Can you give us a general outline of the structure of the department? Also, what was Rob McIntyre's position in the food chain? Was he near the top? Was he active in the departmental politics? Did he have enemies in the department?"

Anni gathered her thoughts for a moment before answering, while she drummed her fingers on her desk, wondering how much she should reveal. She was casually dressed, with a pair of jeans, sneakers, and a soft pastel top completing her ensemble. Attractive earrings dangled from her ears, which made her look not much older than a coed herself. She took a deep breath and began to talk.

"Rob was a full professor. He is, or was, definitely a rising star. He published numerous articles and was working on his third book. He even had a major publisher pick up his second book, which is unusual. His area is an important one, Bioethics. He was in the process of starting a company, with the University as a silent partner. As for enemies, anyone could be jealous of him."

"How about flirtations," Ian asked softly. Anni glanced over at him with a troubled look.

Anni frowned. "I've never heard of anything along those lines, although I don't know a lot of what goes on 'after hours.' I'm afraid you'll have to dig a little deeper on that score."

"Can you introduce us to some of the faculty and staff?" Sam asked. She had her laptop open and was typing furiously, trying to get a better fix on what type of person Rob McIntyre was. "They might have some stories to tell or might know something."

"I can start with the office staff and the Chair of the Department," Anni said, absently twisting a piece of hair around her ear as she spoke. "We'll have to tread lightly. Egos are easily bruised in this environment."

"No time like the present," Ian said under his breath as they entered the main suite.

Bruce Wilkins gazed up at Ian as he shook his hand. Bruce was 5'9" with brown hair, a slightly protruding belly, and the benevolent smile of a contented academic.

"I've heard a lot about you from Anni. I understand you are a musician as well as a private detective, and that you were with the FBI. That's an impressive variety of skills," Bruce said with a smile.

Ian blushed, suddenly unsure of himself in the venerable environment. "I feel like a kid who forgot his homework," he joked, to cover up his discomfort.

Sam decided to cut in. She gave Bruce a smile and modulated her voice to sound like a cop. "I am Sam Peters, Professor Wilkens. It's a pleasure to meet you." Sam stuck out her hand to shake Bruce's, at the same time giving Ian a wink. "You have to pardon Ian…he's not used to the ivory tower."

Bruce steered Sam and Ian into his office, and Anni withdrew to finish the payroll she had started before Sam and Ian's entrance. She looked carefully at the members of her staff for any telltale odd behaviors. She saw several stone faces staring at her with what she took to be curious eyes. She wondered if any of her staff could be involved in any way with the murder. She hoped not…with budgets being cut, anyone involved could be dismissed, and she would probably lose the position. Plus the thought of a murderer or an accomplice outside of her office made her feel nauseous.

Bruce indicated two comfortable chairs in front of his desk, and Sam and Ian sat down. Sam took out her ever-present laptop and hit the on switch. She looked around the office while she waited for the laptop to boot up the Windows menu.

The office held a beautiful view to the lake. Bookshelves lined one wall, and file cabinets occupied the other. A faux-oak desk graced the space in front of the window, with a gray executive swivel chair. There was a low table to one side of the desk made out of the same materials as the desk. It was a comfortable, but not ostentatious space.

"Let's get started, shall we?" Sam smiled at Bruce, who nodded. "We're interesting in getting some background of Professor McIntyre's professional contacts," she began, trying to ease into the interview.

"Rob was a colleague," Bruce said, pulling at his goatee. "I can't imagine why any of our faculty would want him dead. He wasn't a threat to anyone."

"How well did you know Professor McIntyre?" Ian asked, leaning forward and fixed Bruce with a penetrating stare. Bruce looked at Ian, as if sizing up a naughty student. It was a standoff.

"We aren't a terribly large department, so everyone knows each other quite well. Rob had been on campus for ten years. Naturally he attended all the social functions, and departmental meetings. We're sort of like a large family." He shrugged and gave them a small, sad smile.

"Were there any academic competitions that you knew of which might have caused bad feelings towards Professor McIntyre? It sounds like he brought in a lot of research money. Sometimes the successful people in a group are the most despised." Sam threw out the comment to see if she could get a reaction from Bruce. She had liked him immediately, and he seemed very sharp to her. It would help their investigation along to have someone on the inside who could interpret the department politics for them.

"Well," Bruce gave a little laugh. "There are always jealousies. But any dislikes are usually kept on at least a passive-aggressive level. Most people wouldn't commit murder just because someone they work with is a little higher on the ladder. Or would they?" He turned away from Sam and Ian and contemplated the lake. They waited.

"If you could give it some thought and get back to us with any odd interactions you might have noticed, we would appreciate it," Sam said.

Bruce turned back to Sam and Ian. "There is something," he said. "You might check into any investments faculty might have had. I know that Rob was working on something that might have made the use of insulin obsolete. If someone had money invested, and many people do invest in medical companies, there might be something there."

"Do you mean someone may have killed Rob off because they would lose money?" Sam asked incredulously. "It sounds like they would do better to just sell their stocks. Murder seems like solving the problem using a bazooka when a pea shooter would do."

"Maybe you're right. Bruce glanced at his watch. "And now, I have to excuse myself. I have an appointment with a student in two minutes." Bruce led them to the door and shook hands with Ian. "I'm sorry I couldn't be of more help."

"If you think of anything else....anything at all, please call us," Sam said, giving him one of her cards.

"I appreciate all that you are doing. This is a nasty business, and is hurting the morale of the two departments Rob was associated with. God knows we can't afford that kind of bad publicity. I hope you can put an end to this business as soon as possible."

"We'll let you know if we have any further questions. Keep your eyes and ears open, and if you hear anything, please call right away," Sam repeated.

Bruce shoved their card in his pocket absentmindedly and wished them a good day. The door shut and they were left in the main office. Anni came up to them immediately, and the three of them walked outside to wait for an elevator.

"Was he any help?" Anni asked. "Or shouldn't I be asking that question? My my, there was certainly a flurry in the office when you two came in. You'd have thought the Rolling Stones had walked through. I don't know if they know who you are. We aren't talking about people who are exactly experts in the world of rock n' roll here."

"Hmmm," Sam said, her interest quickening. "Do you think any of them know anything?"

"Well, you might be surprised," Anni said. "Sometimes my staff is aware of things about faculty that make me wonder if they have bugs planted in their homes. I guess they tell them things they don't tell me!"

"Another avenue of detection," Sam said, giving Ian a pointed look.

Chapter 11

"So, do we go and eat something and figure out what we know?" Sam joked, thinking of their earlier escapades. They usually hashed over their findings while eating. And it often led to more interesting activities after dinner.

"I dunno," Ian said, running his hands through his hair. They pushed the lobby door open and walked outside of the building. "Why don't we go home and rustle up some food? We can organize what we have, and then…" He wagged his eyebrows at Sam suggestively and let his lips brush against her hair.

"Hey, that's a great idea…how about a nice home-made pizza?" By then Ian's arms were around her and he nuzzled her neck, ignoring the students rushing by as classes changed. They remembered where they were and broke off with embarrassed looks. No one even noticed.

The phone was ringing as they entered the house. Sam rushed to answer it while Ian groaned, and she gave him a disapproving glare.

"Sam, is that you?" Nicole Redding, one half of the leader of Ian's band, *Heartthrob*, demanded from the other end of the line. "How are you guys doing? Are you moved in? Have you gone to classes yet?"

Sam laughed, as she answered the questions one by one. "Yes, it's me. We're fine, although we've already gotten ourselves involved in another murder! How are you guys?! It seems like ages since we've talked to you! What's up? Do you need to talk to Ian?"

"Murder, oh, sweet Jesus!" Nicole yelled into the phone. "I swear you guys are magnets for murder. Say, that might be a fun song to write." Giggles accompanied her statements. "We can't leave you alone for ten minutes! But it is great to hear your voice. I want to hear all about what you've been doing. Did you hook up with your cousin Anni?"

"Indeed," Sam said in answer to all her comments. "What's up? Do you need Ian for something, or do you just miss us?" She wrinkled her eyebrows into a frown, but strove to keep her voice light.

"Well, we booked some studio time. We're wondering if Ian could come up next weekend. Is that going to mess up your investigation?"

"I'll put Ian on," Sam said, not wanting to interfere in any plans the band had made. "You can work it out, I'm sure. If we can't wrap this case before next weekend, I'll carry on by myself." She handed the phone to Ian, who gave her a questioning look. She shrugged as she handed him the phone.

"Hi Nicole! How are the both of you? You must miss the band!" Ian said smoothly, as he winked at Sam. Sam crossed her arms over her chest and waited.

"Okay, if it's all right with Sam, I think I can manage that," Ian said carefully. He covered up the mouthpiece of the phone and whispered to Sam. "I won't go if you think it will interfere with the investigation."

Sam looked at Ian and blinked, thinking furiously. She would rather have him there helping her, but she understood that with the band timing was very important. They needed to get back into the studio and work on their next CD. They could do both things, but it would take careful planning.

She nodded. "Go ahead. I'll manage here without you. We can always call each other on our cell phones. I'll give you updates every day."

Ian uncovered the mouthpiece. "I think that will be all right. If anything big happens, I may have to return to Madison in a hurry. I'll rent a car to drive up there. Then if I have to get home, I'll fly. It's only a forty-minute flight. Yes, I think this will work."

"Great!" Nicole enthused. "Sam is also invited, just in case you crack the case before you come up. It'll be great to get everyone together again. I can't wait! But be careful, we want you both in one piece."

Ian replaced the phone thoughtfully. *Heartthrob* was turning into a big sensation. His role as percussionist gave him some leeway, since he really wasn't in on the song-writing end. He thought the world of Terry and Nicole and would do anything for them.

He turned toward Sam with an uncertain smile. "I hope I haven't bitten off more than I can chew." He also hoped he wouldn't put Sam in danger by leaving a sensitive investigation.

Sam gave him a hug. "We'll make it all work out. Remember, I've handled most of my investigations alone, since my partner in Cleveland had so many marriage problems. I think I'll be in good shape while you're gone. If I need backup, I'll give you a holler.

The rest of the evening was taken up with the home-made pizza, which Sam and Ian worked on together. Sam cut up the vegetables, while Ian smeared pizza sauce on a Boboli crust. With a wink, Ian pulled some shrimp out of the freezer and defrosted it under water. Sam's mouth watered. Shrimp was her favorite food...besides chocolate.

Ian arranged for a rental car for the weekend, and then he and Sam sat down to make some notes.

"Where should we start, boss?" He deferred to Sam's investigative observations, since he wanted to let her gather her thoughts first.

Sam popped open her laptop and waited for the whirring to end, indicating Windows' readiness to accept her contributions. She pursed her lips and frowned at the screen, wondering where to begin.

"So we have a faculty member who is working with Bioethics. That means that he is writing about the morality of cloning, stem-cell research, that type of thing. I think we need to look up some information on what he did. Let's call Janey to see if she can give us some notes. I'll put that on our 'to do' list. We need to check with her next, I think. But let's go back to the interview. There are several motives I can think of off the top of my head. With all the religious fanatics around, Rob's research would make him a major target."

"Do you think there are any local groups who are that extreme? There's also professional jealousy," Ian prompted. "Could Rob have been involved with someone sexually? It shouldn't be hard to count that out, unless something new comes to light. Whom can we talk to about that?"

Sam looked at Ian, and pounded on the keyboard. "That's another item for the 'to do' list. Okay. Was this guy a gambler? Did he take drugs? He almost seems too good to be true. Can you check him out for priors?" She typed furiously, adding to the list.

"How about the financial aspects of research," Ian added, tugging at his curls. "Who donated the money for the research center? Who stood to gain or lose by Rob's death? Did he have any close colleagues? I think we need to go to the Bioethics department. We also need to dig deeper into departmental dynamics in both places."

"I thought Bruce was a bit reticent," Sam murmured. "I can understand the University not wanting us to dig up any skeletons, but on the other hand, they do need to cooperate with us."

"Maybe we should call Anni, and ask her for the dirt on the department. If anyone knows who does what to whom, it would be Anni. I'll add it to the list."

"Let's stop and check the Web for information about Bio-Xen," Ian suggested. "I'm a little hazy about this stuff. All I know is that the Religious Right doesn't want anyone cloning human beings or using tissue for stem-cell research."

They checked the Internet and found various articles dealing with genetic code, describing genomes, chromosomes, genes, and DNA. They learned that there are twenty-three pairs of chromosomes in the nucleus of the body's one hundred trillion cells, and that DNA is a long string in each chromosome. The DNA instructs the cells to do their work, pumping proteins and enzymes throughout the body.

They then checked for information on the Bioethics department, and noted each faculty member and what area of research in which they were engaged. There was a dizzying array of instructors in the areas of medical history, history of science, history of female medicine, history of psychiatry, history of environment, history of health, and history of ethics.

"Fascinating stuff," Sam commented, as she switched from page to page on the website. "I can see why people want to spend their time studying this stuff..."

"Look at that," Ian said, as an article caught their eye. A discussion of the opposition to cloning children and how it would affect legislation in the United States scrolled in front of them. It was a classic case of the scientific community arguing for research to better mankind versus a reluctant and worried public, sensing the possible abuse of power.

"As in Frankenstein," Ian murmured, echoing Sam's thoughts.

Ian checked in with one of his FBI friends via e-mail, but they didn't have anything on Rob. A call to Joel Drake confirmed that the local police didn't have any files other than the murder case under Rob McIntyre's name. Joel suggested they check the CCAP, Wisconsin Circuit Court Access, database. That website provides public access to records of Wisconsin circuit courts for counties involved.

"I don't have time to check CCAP for you," Joel said, "you'll have to do that yourself. They are open records. You just have to check an agreement on the main web page."

They went to the web and found the website. There was nothing there. San scratched her head. There was little that was obvious at first glance to explain the murder of Rob McIntyre. She concentrated and took a deep breath to steady herself, letting the air calm her body and slow her thoughts. Ian waited.

"I wonder if Rob ever received threatening phone calls from religious extremists." Sam finally wondered aloud. "What we've read makes it sound as if Rob's research and new company would be one of their primary targets. Do you think he might have had news coverage that might have served to galvanize the opposition?"

"Maybe," Ian yawned, suddenly overwhelmed. "I vote we stop for the night and engage in more…secular activities…" He eyed Sam before gathering her in his arms, and she nodded sleepily. "Take me to bed, Romeo, and have your way with me…"

Sam woke up a few hours later with her mind spinning in several directions. She left Ian, who was snoring softly, and padded downstairs to make some tea. She found that Chamomile tea with honey and peppermint took the edge off when a case was bothering her.

She sat down at the kitchen table to sip her tea and think. She didn't think that Rob McIntyre had been killed by a jealous lover. So far his biotech company seemed like the best place to begin investigating. It could be one of two scenarios: either someone else on the faculty was jealous of McIntyre's research or had a financial reason to be angry at him. Of course there were always the right-wing nuts, as Sam liked to think of them.

When she had been in Cleveland she had taken a homicide investigation where an abortion doctor had been gunned down by a fanatic. It had been an ugly case that had involved several churches, and it had shaken Sam to see that kind of behavior in the United States.

Sam believed in the principle of Occam's razor, the idea that the fewest possible assumptions should be made in explaining a thing. Some people believe that that means the first explanation that comes to mind is usually the correct one. In Sam's experience, that was dangerous thinking. She preferred to think of it as keeping an open mind until the facts presented themselves into a logical order.

She sighed and finished her tea. She had a feeling that this case was going to be anything but simple. It was time to go to bed. No doubt tomorrow would be better.

Chapter 12

The next morning Janey McIntyre called to tell them she was faxing notes about faculty members from both departments. Sam ran to turn on her computer and impatiently waited for the fax to arrive. She didn't have to stare at the printer for long...less than ten minutes later the machine spit out five pages.

In typical English teacher fashion, Janey had each faculty member typed in bold, followed by a paragraph with their specialty area, a short biography, personality characteristics, and her opinion as to whether they might be involved in the murder.

"Whew! That's a lot of names to run down," Ian complained, as he scanned forty-six names. "But this should come in very handy."

"Our next step is to visit the Bioethics office," Sam murmured.

"Yes, it's time to check out the other department," Ian agreed. "But I want to run these names through the FBI computer to see if anyone has a record. I still haven't worn out my welcome with the Bureau...I hope. Never know what might turn up."

The Bioethics department occupied a small portion of one of the University research buildings. There were only five faculty members and one administrator in a chunk of ten offices. The faculty members each had their own office. The administrator, whose name was Betty Brown, sat in a two-room suite. One room held the copier and postage meter, and Betty occupied an office which contained a desk, several filing cabinets, a computer telephone, and a couple of chairs. She had graced the Spartan environment with plants, photographs of her family, and a candy dish which she kept filled with M & M's.

Betty was in her early fifties, with a chin-length blunt haircut that made her brown hair look unassuming. She had large, brown eyes which were lovely and a welcoming smile with even, white teeth. She was dressed in casual navy slacks and a button-down white oxford shirt. She wore a chunky turquoise necklace and earrings to match from one of her Arizona vacations.

"You must be Sam and Ian." She gave them a bright smile that faded when she remembered the purpose of their visit. "I just can't believe someone would do such a horrible thing to Professor McIntyre. He was the nicest faculty member here, and his wife and children are just darling. I hope you can find out who did this to him." Her eyes shone with tears.

Sam and Ian gave her a moment to compose herself. As she took a deep breath and reached for a tissue, the sun shone into her office creating a warm atmosphere, which in contrast to the mood of the visit. Sam looked outside at branches blowing in a gentle breeze. This murder seemed to ripple out as their investigation continued.

She gave Betty a gentle smile. "We'll try our best. We're hoping you can give us an idea of your faculty and their jobs. The more information we have, the easier our investigation will be."

Betty dabbed at her eyes with a tissue and then wadded it angrily into a ball and gave a sniff, trying to get herself back together. "I can't imagine any of our faculty would be involved. They can be difficult…faculty are trained to work in a solitary environment. They often clash at faculty meetings over political issues, but I can't believe that anything that is discussed would lead to murder."

Sam and Ian looked at each other. This was going to be tough going. It was obvious that university personnel were unaccustomed to dealing with anything as sordid as murder.

"Are there any issues that you know of that would involve a considerable sum of money?" Ian asked, giving Betty his best version of a bedside manner.

Betty eyes searched Ian's, looking for an answer. "Nothing other than the usual research grants." Her voice shook as she tried to regain control.

"Could anyone have killed Professor McIntyre to seize control of his new company?" Sam asked, thinking in a new direction.

Betty's frowned. "No one on the immediate faculty would be involved, I shouldn't think. They all have their own research interests...you know, History of Science, feminine medicine, European medicine, history of the med sciences, that sort of thing. As I said before, each faculty member carves out his or her own territory. It would have to be something else that would provide a motive for murder." She shuddered. "I don't feel safe myself. The murderer could be anyone...a student, a graduate student with a grudge, someone who doesn't agree with stem cell research."

"Have your office received any written threats?" Sam asked, swinging her gaze from the window she had been staring out of, hands clasped behind her back, to Betty. She turned around to give Betty her full attention.

Betty blanched, remembering. "Yes, we have," she said softly, her voice tightening. "We didn't think anything of it at the time...chalked it up to some religious nutcase." She took a sip of water to clear her throat.

"Do you have a copy of the note?" Sam continued, her voice sympathetic at Betty's obvious distress.

Betty walked over to the file cabinet, pulled it open, and started thumbing through the files. "It should be here. I labeled the file something having to do with threats. I sure didn't think much of it at the time. I can't remember exactly what. Oh, here it is. I had it filed under "Crank Letters."

One never knows when a letter might match a deed." She smiled at them sadly as she handed the file over.

Sam opened the file and read it out loud for Ian's benefit:

"Dear Professor McIntyre. It has come to our attention that you are engaging in highly suspicious research involving stem cells. Or you know the parties who are engaging in this research. This research is against the laws of nature, and as such, our church, the Church of the New Order, considers you an enemy. Cease and desist your research immediately, or face the consequences."

"It was not signed," Betty sighed. "It could be anyone." She shook her head. "I wish I had paid more attention. Maybe I should have called the police."

"May we take this for fingerprinting?" Sam asked. "I imagine there are several sets of prints, but maybe something will emerge that might prove interesting."

"Be my guest," Betty slapped the letter into Sam's hand. "I'll do anything I can to help with your investigation. This is creeping everyone out around here. We want it solved."

Sam placed the file in her briefcase. "If there is anything else you can think of, let us know. Try to remember anyone in the department who you think might have had an argument with Professor McIntyre. Anything, no matter how small, would help."

Betty reached for another tissue. "I'll wrack my brain. We do get many people in here. Sometimes we have researchers come in for a semester. I'll make up a list and fax it to you." She accepted a card from Sam and muttered: "I hope you catch the son-of-a-bitch."

* * * * *

"Time to call Marie Cavendish," Sam said, as they left Betty's office. She punched in a telephone number she had written in haste on her wrist before they left the Philosophy Department. Anni had looked up the number for her and Sam didn't want to lose it.

The line rang five times before an answering machine clicked on with Marie Cavendish's voice. "Hi, this is Marie. You know the drill. I'll call you as soon as I can." Her voice sounded young and buoyant.

"Marie, this is Sam Peters, a private detective. My partner, Ian Temple, and I would very much like to talk to you about the death of Professor Rob McIntyre." Sam left her cell phone and home phone numbers and broke the connection.

"Damn," she said. "I hope she calls us soon. She is the only witness and could maybe tell us something that we've missed. I wonder where she is."

Chapter 13

"I wondered when I was gonna hear from you again," Joel Drake drawled when they called on him that afternoon. "I suppose you have something else you'd like our overworked lab to take a look at... huh?"

Ian grinned as he handed the bagged letter over. "You took the words right out of my mouth, Joel. Actually, this letter came from Betty Brown's office over at the Department of Bioethics. We'd be mighty obliged if you could test it for fingerprints."

Joel gave an exasperated grown. "I suppose it's a crank letter the department's had lying around for a while, and it's probably full of smeared prints."

"You got it. It's probably nothing, but we like to be thorough. Could your lab find time to do this for us?"

Joel hesitated only a second, as he thought about what tactic to take with the people in the lab. Maybe Shannon would do it...she owed him a few favors. "All right, I think I can twist some arms to get this done for you."

"Has anything else come up we should know about?" Sam asked. She felt a sudden tingle as a surprised expression crossed Joel's features. There was something there.

Joel was impressed. Sam was quite a detective, and she had picked up on the latest development. This didn't really concern them, but he decided to share what he had.

"There's been another death," he said quietly. "And we didn't even get to interview her, other than the morning of the murder."

Sam was grim. "Is it Marie Cavendish?"

"That's right. That means whoever murdered Rob McIntyre stayed close enough to the scene to watch someone find the body. I think we're looking for a man here. It had to be someone big and strong. Perhaps it was another jogger. Or someone who used the disguise of a jogger to get close enough to Rob McIntyre to kill him."

Sam shivered, thinking over the possibilities. "We might be dealing with a serial killer. Did she die the same way?"

"Yep," Joel said, shaking his head.

"Where did it happen?"

"In front of her house, she was working late in a lab and was attacked on her way home. She made it as far as her front steps. He must have been waiting for her."

"Oh oh, this might be another case where the reporters will swarm over the police and maybe us. If we're dealing with a serial killer, he might look our way."

"We'll keep a low profile," Ian cut in, eyes steely.

"We haven't been noticed by the press yet," Sam noted, frowning. "If we can keep our investigation secret, we might be all right."

Joel nodded in agreement. "Your investigation has already been very helpful to the department. We'll keep a lid on your involvement. Who knows what you'll be able to turn up. You won't be constrained by the rules and regulations we have. Yes, I think this might work out very well. Just don't take any unnecessary chances. We don't want to have to come and scrape you two off the sidewalk."

Chapter 14

Joel Drake frowned once again at the letter Sam produced in its plastic bag. He had decided that they needed some additional briefing, so he had asked them to stick around while he made some phone calls. They reassembled in his office a half hour later. Ian sat in his chair, his feet splayed out in front of him. Sam played with a tendril of her red hair while her mind raced.

"I think this might be a fool's errand, but we'll check this out," he murmured more to himself than to Sam and Ian, since the procedure had already been decided upon.

Joel sat at a regulation Badger State Industry desk, which had been assembled by prison inmates twenty-five years earlier. His vinyl chair had a big crack in the back. The neutral linoleum on his floor bore matching scars to those on the back of his chair. The fluorescent lighting would have been blinding if some of the light bulbs hadn't been judiciously unscrewed to cut the glare, a common practice among government employees.

Sam looked out the window, to find relief from the institutional setting. A gentle breeze blew branches of the mature maples and oaks that surrounded the building, floating the branches in the wind. It was another beautiful almost fall day with silky sunshine and wispy clouds punctuating the blue sky. Sam sat up straight to stretch out her spine and exhaled slowly to east her tension.

"We have to start somewhere. At least we can eliminate possibilities. Do you have any record of any deranged characters who hang around the University? If there were any police records, we could at least investigate that avenue and spare you the trouble."

Joel gave them a tight smile. "We'd be stupid not to allow you to follow some of these leads. We're always undermanned these days. We're fighting budget cuts, the incursion of gangs into our fair city, and self-serving politicians." He let his breath out in a sigh.

"Sometimes I wonder why I'm in this racket. I was a football player when I went through school here. But I wrecked my knee." He started, remembering where he was. His mind had been on the football field. "I would have gone pro, but you know how it goes."

Ian nodded in understanding. He had played football in college himself and had toyed with a professional career, but couldn't quite make the cut. "Life can hand us all sorts of curve balls," he commented softly. He liked this big man and saw strength of character that fit in with his own ideals of what people should strive for in their lives.

"Say, Joel," Ian abruptly changed the subject. "I have to go to the Twin Cities this weekend for some recording with *Heartthrob*. I'm reluctantly leaving Sam behind. If she needs any help, I'm hoping you'll be there for her."

"You're not asking me to baby-sit..." Joel began, dark eyes flashing.

"Oh, no, nothing like that," Sam said hastily. "I just want to be able to call if anything comes up...one never knows in this business. I...that is we... wanted to give you a heads up in case. Probably won't happen...I hope." She gave Joel her brightest smile.

"Oh, I get ya," Joel said, realization dawning across his features. "You mean if you catch our man, you'll want someone to formally arrest him."

"Yeah, a little backup," Sam said with a small smile. "Just in case..."

"Okay," Joel said, "but we need to lay some ground rules right now. First, you call me at the first sign of trouble. I know you two worked in law enforcement, but I don't want something to go wrong which would turn into a lawsuit. Second, remember this is a high profile, university related case. This is a company town, if you know what I mean. Everyone is connected. The University is a big employer, and we can't afford any scandals. Third, don't engage unless you are acting in self defense. If you think you've got the bad guy, call me immediately. We can have someone there in minutes. And finally, don't do anything to put Anni in danger, or I'll skin your hides. Understood?"

Sam and Ian gave a simultaneously salute. "Yes, sir." they said in unison.

"Well, that went well," Ian commented as they walked out the door. Sam cracked up, remembering that Ian had made the exact same comment the first time they had met her boss, Jerry Malone. Jerry had dressed Ian down in the same manner. It was beginning to feel like a common reaction. Ian scratched his head, baffled.

"We're not wearing the uniform anymore," Sam explained, sensing Ian's thoughts. "It makes a big difference, and even if we're thought well of, the authorities have to put constraints on what we do."

"Well, it makes me feel like a cadet again," Ian commented, referring to his training days. "And you know how I feel about school."

"Yup, I do," Sam answered. "Come on, we've got things to do, especially if you're going to abandon me for a few days."

Chapter 15

Ian reluctantly gave Sam a dutiful kiss, then squeezed her and lingered a little longer. He wanted to make sure she missed him...a lot.

"Not fair," Sam laughed, after they broke apart. "You just want me to go along, where you can watch me." Ian's guilty look told her she had found the brass ring.

"It's not quite that," Ian began gingerly, not wanting to anger her into action. "I'd just feel better if I could be here. Or you could come with me."

"Don't worry," Sam said cheerfully. "I have Anni. The two of us played detectives when we were little. We're just going to poke around a little. We're not going to solve this case unless we take some action that the police can't."

"What do you have in mind?" Ian queried.

"I want to check out the professor with the weapons. He's another suspect we could possibly eliminate. He's most likely just an innocent sweetie who doesn't know what to do with his money, but we have to know for sure."

"You'll keep in touch?"

Sam patted her cell phone and her gun. "Oh yeah, I'll keep in touch. Just go and lay down your tracks and come back to me as soon as you can." Ian simply needed to record his part to fit in with what the band had already laid down on tape. It was a relatively quick procedure. "And give my love to everyone. And get a date for that wedding, so we can plan our schedule!"

"Yes, ma'am," Ian gave her a solemn salute. "I will not fail you...on all counts."

Ian turned to walk down the concourse. New airport security prevented Sam from accompanying him to the gate, so she turned to find an exit out of the Dane County Airport and retrieve their van from the parking lot. She had an hour to pick up Anni, go to lunch to plot strategy, and carry out their mission.

Anni tapped her foot nervously as she waited for Sam. Their plan was to lunch at the Imperial Gardens, organize their watch for the weekend, and carry out their plans. This was a big change of pace for Anni...she devoured mysteries and remembered childhood escapades with Sam, but wondered if she was up to catching a killer.

Sam pulled up just as Anni was losing her nerve. Her face was bright with the chase, and Anni forgot her reservations. She felt like a disciple, and she was determined not to let her department and her cousin down.

"Hi Anni, are you ready for Undercover Work 101?" Sam quipped. She gave Anni a radiant smile and patted the seat next to her.

Anni took a fortifying breath and got into the car. "Damn straight. Let's go find out who is killing my friends." Her face set itself into hard lines and her eyes turned into the mirrors of an enforcer.

"Great. Now let's go eat and regroup, and then we'll go kick some butt," Sam replied, giving her cousin a shark grin.

Chapter 16

"So, have you done any more thinking about your faculty?" Sam looked over at Anni, as they drove to the "older" west side neighborhood of Madison. Many of the professors were clumped there in old, overpriced houses in various states of repair.

"Other than Fred Canon, I can't think of anyone else who might have a motive at the moment," Anni answered thoughtfully. She felt uncomfortable and wondered if they were going on a wild goose chase. She suddenly felt that she was wrongfully intruding into the life of someone she worked with. She didn't feel that it was right.

Sam read her thoughts. "This is important, Anni. There's been a murder…actually two murders. I know that what we're doing probably goes against your principles, but we simply have to check out some suspects."

"I know," Anni agreed reluctantly. "Maybe I'm not cut out for detective work…"

"Give it some time…don't pass judgment before we've achieved our objective," Sam laughed. She gave Anni a reassuring glance. "It'll be a piece of cake…really…"

"Shouldn't we just go talk to him? I mean, if the guy has an alibi for the night of the murder."

"All right," Sam said. "There's a car in the driveway. Let's go and ask some questions, if you are comfortable with that idea."

"How about if I stay in the car," Anni said nervously. "I don't want to get into trouble with the department."

"Okay, I'll go to the door and talk to him," Sam said. She opened the van and strode to the door, pushing on the doorbell. After a few minutes the door was opened by a middle aged man with balding brown hair and a runner's slim build.

Sam talked to the professor for a few minutes, and suddenly he shut the door in her face. She blinked at the affront, and after a moment turned around and walked back to the van, deep in thought.

"The good professor didn't want to talk to me," she told Anni when she reached the van. "I think we should stick around and do a little surveillance on his house. There's something odd going on here."

"Okay, but I just hope no one recognizes me," Anni said gloomily. She looked around nervously. "Faculty stick together, and if someone saw us, I'd never live it down." She took a deep breath. "Oh well, no guts, no glory. Did you say two murders?!"

Sam looked at Anni soberly. "Yeah, the woman who found Dr. McIntyre was murdered on her front steps. It's the same modus operandi." She looked grim. "So, the stakes have increased. We have to solve this case!"

They settled in to wait outside the modest Cape Cod style home. Sam thought it was perfect for an "absent-minded professor." There were two huge blue spruce trees standing guard like sentries, ready to question any intruders. The house itself was brick on the bottom with white siding on top. The small lawn was precisely cut, attesting to some attention to detail, and the spruce trees were also perfectly trimmed. A beige, older model Nissan sat in the driveway.

"He isn't married, correct?" Sam looked over at Anni for an affirmative answer, and Anni nodded her head.

"What'll we do now?"

"Just wait. I brought some chocolate, chips, water, and sodas, or if you want, some fruit. It could be a long afternoon."

They settled down, at first munching their treats, but then realized that the more they ate, the sooner they'd need to make a rest stop. "I refuse to pee in a jar!" Anni declared indignantly, "I'd rather hold it!" That brought a laugh, and they once again settled down.

Nothing happened for two hours. Restless and cramped, Anni began to grumble. "I don't know if this was such a good idea, Sam" as another car drove up to the house. Sam and Anni quickly ducked down, hoping they hadn't been spotted.

"Another faculty member," Anni observed, lifting her head just enough to take a peek.

"Who is it?" Sam asked gently, not wanting to push.

"Well, I'll be darned," Anni declared. "It's Susan Hilger. They are about the same age; both are single. Maybe they have something going on." She sat up a little straighter, craning her head around for a better look.

Susan Hilger stood about 5'7" tall, and had a slender figure for her forty-five years. She had sparkling brown eyes and brown hair blunt cut to her chin. She wore jeans, a light pullover, and running shoes. She carried a few CD's and DVD's in her hands and a bunch of freshly cut flowers of varying sizes and colors. She also carried a bottle of wine, and her expression was one of sheer anticipation.

"Now I feel like I'm really intruding," Anni murmured, entranced. "But those are the tools for a romantic interlude, or I'll eat my hat. Funny, I never pictured those two together."

"Well, I think we've got some answers, at least for the time being," Sam declared. The front door once again stood ajar, and as they stood on the porch Susan had given her professor a peck on the cheek. He had whispered something in her ear, which produced some merriment.

"Can't we go now?" Anni pleaded when the door once again shut. "I would hate to have them catch us. I think we can imagine what is going on in there."

"Well, at least we've established one romantic pairing," Sam commented wryly as she switched on the ignition and pulled on to the street, much to Anni's relief.

Chapter 17

"Whew! I'm glad that's over," Anni murmured as they drove in search of a restaurant. They decided to stop at Quiznos for a sub sandwich. Anni opted for vegetarian; Sam had a turkey and ham mixed with lots of greens. They both crunched in delight and relief, after having used the restroom. "So, where do we go from here? I don't have a clue..." They both laughed at the pun.

"I think it's time to check in with your favorite ex-football great," Sam offered. "I also want to call Janey, to make sure she's all right and to see if she has any new ideas for us. She's had some time to think, and she might have remembered something." She pulled out her cell phone and dialed, asking for Detective Joel Drake."

"Detective Drake, this is Sam Peters. Is there anything new happening on your end? No, Anni and I just finished a stakeout, but nothing turned up. I'm afraid we're at a dead end, but I have some ideas." Her brow furrowed as she listened. "Okay, keep in touch."

"Nothing, a big zero," Sam grabbed her hair with both hands and stared at her empty plate. Anni looked on helplessly. She felt that she should know something. She wracked her brain trying to come up with ideas.

"Maybe we should go through the faculty list again," she offered hopefully. "There's got to be something we've missed."

"Said like a true detective," Sam laughed, touching Anni lightly on the arm. If nothing else, it felt good to be spending time with her cousin again. But she didn't want to put her in danger or jeopardize her position at the University by asking too many questions. She felt certain the answer was there, but she just couldn't see it.

"I know it's related to the University," she said in frustration. "I'll be glad when Ian gets back. I'm used to working with a partner. We bounce ideas back and forth. It's weird having to share Ian with the band, although I love that part of his personality."

Anni looked at Sam sympathetically. "Don't worry about my position at the University," she laughed. "As long as we don't accuse a dean or the chair of the department, we should be all right. It can get very political there, though."

Sam looked up at Anni and bit her lower lip. "Exactly, it's got to be something related to politics. I think we need to go over your 'big cheeses' to figure it out."

"Janey," they both said at once. Sam brought out her cell phone once more and dialed Janey's number after looking it up in her address book.

"Hello," Janey's formal, sad schoolteacher voice answered.

"Janey, this is Sam. Look, we were just thinking about the politics once more. Have you come up with anything?" Sam listened intently, drumming fingers on the table. She pulled out a notebook and started scribbling madly. Anni watched her intently until the conversation finally came to an end. Sam turned off her phone, snapped her notebook shut, and looked at Anni.

"What?" Anni demanded, as Sam wrinkled her brow and pursed her lips.

"We have more shadowing to do," Sam replied. "No time like the present. Do you have to make another pit stop before we take off?"

"Where are we going this time?" Anni asked breathlessly after she scrambled to the bathroom and ran back to where Sam was waiting.

"We'll be doing surveillance on Phyllis Litchfield and Tom Jacobs. They are the philosophy power couple.

They're married. In fact, they were hired on what's called a "spousal hire." They are not very popular in the department, but they co-authored a book on ethics together which hit the bestseller list. So they can't really be touched. They've been on the local news and even the Today Show. Their big thing is hitting on marriage as an institution that no longer is viable in our society. Kind of ironic, don't you think?"

"So, why are we tailing them?" Anni asked. She felt very nervous about this latest development because she was terrified of the duo. They had given her a hard time in the past, and she tried to stay as far away from them as possible.

"Because today is 'tail 'em day,'" Sam laughed. "We probably won't find anything earth shattering. I just want to get a feel for these two."

Anni took another deep breath. She felt a little like she was suffocating. "All right, but I'm ducking down at any sign of movement. They just live a few blocks from here. Let's go."

Two more hours of surveillance yielded the couple leaving their residence and coming back with groceries. "A normal enough activity," Sam remarked. "But I wouldn't expect them to come out with signs on their heads. But at least I know what they look like. Let's head for home and call Ian."

Anni sighed with relief. "I'm with you. Let's go." Anni started having some doubts about whether she belonged in this investigation. She loved her job at the Department of Philosophy and felt that the privacy of her professors was being compromised. However, there had been a murder. It changed everything.

Anni shivered as she thought of the implications of what had happened. No one in Philosophy was safe until the murderer was caught. The situation would breed suspicion and undermine morale in the department.

She stared glumly out the window as Sam drove. Sam looked over at her cousin and instantly sensed her mood. She had seen the same reaction many times in the course of her murder investigations. The killer was having an impact on not only the victim and their family, but everyone in the victim's world.

"Hey, are you okay?" Sam asked her cousin softly.

Anni looked over at Sam miserably, tears beginning to course down her cheeks. She didn't say anything as her emotions swirled in her head.

"We just have to solve this murder, Sam. It'll destroy the faculty. Right now this bastard has the upper hand." Anni stuck out her chin, reminding Sam of her own reactions when she was upset.

"Don't worry, Anni. We'll get this murderer. It'll take some work, but we won't fail." Sam stuck her chin out in the same way as her cousin as they both thought of the task ahead of them. They saw each other's chins and laughed at the family resemblance.

Chapter 18

Ian usually loved recording. The studio was a great place to just relax and let the creative juices flow. The engineer sat patiently in the sound booth, playing the tracks the band had already laid down for their newest song, "Hooked on You."

Ian listened intently, playing with his percussion instruments and trying various beats to surround the lyrics, which were up-tempo. He'd developed his style by listening to movie soundtracks. Ian was a total movie fanatic. He loved the plots, but his sensitive ear zoned in on the music. He'd even been allowed to sit in on orchestra sessions as a kid because his uncle played violin. Ian loved the world of music. It made him feel alive and in tune with his being. It made him tingle.

But today he felt distracted. He wondered how Sam and Anni were progressing with their stakeout. He felt like he should be there with them, and impatiently tried to rush his part. When the engineer played back what he had just laid down, Ian flushed with embarrassment.

"Sorry, I guess my mind wasn't with that take. Do you mind if we take a little break? I'd like to make a call." When Randy the engineer gave a nod and a smile, Ian darted out in the hallway and pulled out his cell phone. He pushed buttons quickly, feeling his pulse quicken. He hoped everything was fine and that he was worrying needlessly.

"Sam, are you all right?" He tried to keep his voice from betraying his anxiety.

"Of course we're all right," Sam answered softly, trying to reassure Ian. "I wish you were here, because I need your thinking on this. And I just need you in general."

"I'm having a hard time with this session. I'm too distracted, I guess," Ian answered, reassured. "What did you find out?"

"Well, we've discovered a love affair. That's about it. There is another 'power couple' I've found out about. I don't know if they figure into all this. Other than that, I don't have much to report." Sam sounded discouraged.

"I'll make it home as soon as I can. Love you too." He folded his phone thoughtfully and put it back in his pocket.

"Trouble in paradise," Nicole asked, walking up to him. She wasn't being facetious; her face was a mask of concern.

"What?" Ian turned as she walked up to him. "Oh no, nothing like that," he answered absentmindedly.

"I think you'd better fill us in on what's going on...perhaps after the session?" Nicole pressed gently. "Maybe we can help you come up with some answers."

"I'd like that," Ian smiled at Nicole. Nicole was his second favorite female in the world, right behind Sam.

The rest of the session went smoothly with Ian nailing his part. He almost forgot the murder for that precious time that he was creating his part on the latest song.

Nicole and Terry called the entire band together for a combination luncheon and band meeting. Eating was the first order of business, and the Italian restaurant they chose fit the bill perfectly. Nicole opted for tortellini with meatballs, while Terry and Ian shared a pizza.

Jake Ross tore into his own medium pizza, with cheese, sausage, and mushrooms. His drummer fingers tapped on the table as he wolfed down his pizza.

"Are you writing a song there, partner?" Rick Hunter, Jake's best friend and the bass player in *Heartthrob* inquired innocently. Rick was always teasing Jake about one thing or another. Jake was so brilliant and mellow that nothing bothered him, and he genuinely liked Rick's lame attacks.

"What? Do you want me to figure out your bass part for ya too?" Jake returned the jibe with a smile on his face. Rick pretended to be hurt, and then he and Jake cracked up.

"I do have some information to give you about the wedding," Jake announced proudly. The wedding he referred to was that of Patty Boyd and Robert Pierce. Patty and Robert took over the booking agency after Ridley and his partner's demise. Robert and Patty's wedding was planned in two months, and *Heartthrob* had agreed to play at the wedding dance.

"Ah, do tell!" Nicole gasped, excited. "This is gonna be one heckuva shindig!"

"You're right about that," Jake announced proudly. The guest list is 500 people long and growing."

"If it gets much bigger, we'll need a coliseum to play in," Rick Hunter chimed in. "Maybe the Target Center would be available!" *Heartthrob* had played at the Target Center when the murder of Ridley was solved and their fate sealed as a big name band.

"We just may have to do that. Patty is really excited about the band playing. She's even putting out a press release to go out with the wedding invitations!"

"So, that's our next daunting challenge?" Rick inquired. Rick was a total sword and sorcery nut. He'd seen "The Lord of the Rings" trilogy countless times and owned all the relevant DVD's, CD's, posters and even some gear from the movies.

"We'll be counting on it, Rick," Nicole said with a smile.

"And, now, on to Ian," Terry said, taking over the conversation and eyeing Ian meaningfully. "We'd like to hear about your present case...eh, that is, as much as you can tell us. Maybe we can be of some help."

Ian gave Terry a grateful look. The case was beginning to eat at him, and he found that he *did* want to talk about it. "I can only give you sketchy details, you understand. Confidentiality and all that applies here..."

"But it's a murder case...right?" Nicole broke in. "I think I know which one it is...I read about it in the paper. What can you tell us about it without breaching ethics?"

"We're just in the preliminary stages of the investigation, really," Ian replied. "Sam's cousin Anni works at the University, and she's been helping us with the investigation. That's what bothers me. I don't want to put the woman I love and her family into danger. So I've been worried about it."

"Why don't you invite Sam and Anni up to Minneapolis for a few days? Heck, we solved one case up here...maybe something will turn up. But in the meantime you can hit some restaurants, get more recording done, and you can give your brain a rest for a few days."

"We are sort of stalled at the moment," Ian answered, running his fingers through his hair absentmindedly.

"Maybe you're right. We certainly should do something for Anni...she's been such a help. I don't think they let her out of her cage very often down there. She'd probably jump at the chance. I'll call Sam right now."

Ian redialed Sam's number and presented her with the new plan.

"What a great idea!" Sam said enthusiastically. "I'd just love to go back to the Mall...we didn't spend enough time there to suit me the last trip. We could also hit some restaurants. I'd bet that Anni would love to get away too. She's been stressing over this case."

"Great!" Ian said. "Why don't you give Anni a call and present our idea to her and see if she can get off work for a few days. Promise her anything. I really would feel much better if I had the two of you close enough to keep an eye on." He listened for a negative reaction.

There was a silence on the other end of the phone as Sam thought over the idea. She was a little worried about leaving, but understood that Ian was needed there with the recording. "Okay, I'll call you back in five." The phone went dead.

Four and a half minutes later Ian's cell phone played a Mozart ditty and he picked it up. "What did she say? Will she do it? She will? Fantastic!"

After listening for a few minutes, Ian clicked off and turned to the others. "They're both coming...driving up in our van. They should be here by tomorrow afternoon." The worry lines around his face smoothed out a little and he let out a slow breath.

Rick, Jake and Terry looked at Ian meaningfully. He smiled back at them and shook his head, indicating that he couldn't tell them any more about the case. They sighed and returned to their pizzas, pretending indifference.

Finally Terry broke the silence. "Ian, if there is anything that we can do to make this easier for you, just say the word. You know how we all feel about you, and we'd do anything to help you out, buddy."

Ian flashed Terry a grateful smile. "Thanks, bro. I know it, and your friendship means everything to me. I'll do my best at this recording session. I won't let you down. As for the case, we'll call you if we need anything. I guess I was just worrying about leaving Sam and Anni alone with that murderer running around loose. If that guy who did this catches wind of the fact that we are investigating, there is no telling what he might do. I have a feeling this is one bad dude."

There was silence around the table as the band thought of the ramifications of Ian's speech. They understood how dangerous his work could be, and thoughts of what could happen quelled their enthusiasm."

"We'll make their trip worthwhile," Nicole finally said, giving Ian's arm a squeeze. She didn't know how right she would be.

Chapter 19

A call to their landlady confirmed that she would take care of their critters, so Sam felt good about leaving them. They wouldn't have to go to a vet clinic and stay in a cage. Cleo and Quincy were winding around her legs as she put in the call to their landlady, Sue Cullin.

"I love kitties! I'd be happy to take care of them," Sue said enthusiastically when Sam posed the question to her. "I can come over for instructions if you like. I'm dying to see how many boxes you've unpacked! Are you going 'undercover' or doing something with an investigation? I never knew any private detectives before…or famous musicians!"

"Great! Can you come over tonight? We're planning on leaving in the morning. I'm sure the kitties will hide while we're gone. They are still getting used to this place. Just make sure they don't run outside…they wouldn't last long in the traffic. We don't let them out at all. And, we still have a few boxes to unpack, here and there…"

"How about 7:00 p.m.? I should have some time then. Oh, this is such fun!"

A call to Anni produced a similar result, and Sam began to feel more relaxed about leaving. *I'd better give Janey McIntyre a call…just to make sure everything is all right on that end.* She sat on the couch and two kitties immediately jumped up for scritching (cat scratching) while she dialed the phone.

Janey McIntyre answered almost immediately. "Sam, is that you? Do you have any news for me? I've been a nervous wreck!"

77

Sam bit her lip. She hoped Janey wouldn't react negatively to her trip. "Janey, yes, it's me. I just wanted to let you know that both Ian and I will be out of town for a couple of days."

"Oh," Janey said with a twinge of surprise. "Does the case lead you out of town? I would have thought that you'd have enough to do here as it is."

"That's why I'm calling," Sam said. "I wondered if you knew of any visiting faculty who might be from the University of Minnesota. Ian is recording with the band up there, and I thought I would check on that end if there are any connections."

"I'm not sure," Janey said. "Let me call Bioethics and find out. I'll call you right back."

After signing off from Janey, Sam put in a call to Joel Drake. She was beginning to feel a little nervous about the trip. Maybe she shouldn't go. But since Ian was there she wanted to make it work. She felt torn, and her stomach churned in reaction to her indecision.

Joel answered the phone in his usual brusque manner. Sam smiled to herself when she heard the tone. She loved irascible teddy bears...Joel reminded her of her former boss and mentor, Jerry Malone. She made a mental note to also call Jerry.

"Sam Peters here, Joel. I just wanted to let you know that Ian and I will be out of town for the next three days. If anything comes up, I wanted to give you my cell phone number."

"Sam!" Joel's voice boomed. "Nothing much is happening with the case at the moment. We're still waiting for possible fingerprints on your "crank" letter. We're also keeping a watch on Janey's house. Yes, I'd appreciate having you just a call away at all times."

Sam looked out the window at storm clouds that were ominously gathering outside her window, threatening humanity with a good pelting. Shades of black and grey commingled with rolling thunder, reminding her of a cavalry gathering for battle. She could feel a sinus headache beginning and wondered if it was a portent of something to come. She tore her eyes away from the window and tried to focus on what Joel was saying.

"Are you tearing off after a clue, or just running away for a couple of days?" Joel joked.

"Ian is recording with the band. He wants me up there, so I figured if I need to make the trip, I would check out any leads that might require research there. Do you know of any faculty who might have connections to the University of Minnesota?"

"Hmmm, it might take some work to make that connection," Joel responded wearily. "Do you really think there might be something there?"

"It's possible," Sam replied. "I just don't want to lose contact with any new developments here. And if I'm there, I'd just as soon get some results for my time."

Joel was impressed in spite of himself. Sam was a straight shooter, and he could see why Anni thought so much of her cousin. Sam lived up to her reputation.

"I'll see what I can turn up. I may not have anything for you before you leave," he warned.

"I understand," Sam replied. "Just give me a call on my cell if anything turns up."

She punched the off button on her phone and tapped her finger on the on the dining room table for a few minutes while her thoughts raced. There was something here…she could feel it. It seemed rational to check on connections with other universities in the area. The idea opened up many possibilities. She decided to call Jerry Malone.

For the second time that day Sam heard the gruff voice of someone she highly respected, "Malone here."

"Got some time for an old friend?" Sam asked softly.

"Red, great to hear from ya," Malone roared into the phone so that Sam had to hold the receiver six inches from her traumatized ear. "What's up kid? Don't tell me you're involved in another murder! I thought you and Ian would relax for a few weeks!"

"Well, your ability to cut to the chase hasn't changed," Sam said affectionately. "And, yes, we are involved in, as you put it, another murder."

"Not the two in Madison I read about?" Jerry chuckled, knowing Sam would be impressed with his knowledge.

"Well, I can't say, but you're close," Sam admitted. "So far we've hit a brick wall. My cousin Anni and I are going up to Minneapolis to join Ian for a few days. I'm going to snoop around there while Ian is busy."

"Well, you certainly have good luck finding things in that city. Maybe you'll have a command performance." Jerry chuckled at his own pun.

"Well, it's a frustrating case. Whoever the killer is, he's professionally trained. It's hard to balance that with people who seem to be pacifists," Sam commented.

Jerry nodded his head sympathetically on the other end. He was silent for a few moments while he digested the implications of what Sam said. In his experience it was especially difficult to solve murders at universities. Too many people were involved, and too many smoke screens went up.

"Can you tell me which department is involved?"

"Bioethics," Sam answered, wondering why he was asking.

"That would be where I'd concentrate the investigation if I were you," he offered.

"That's what I've thought all along. Maybe there is some connection with a startup company here." Sam scratched two kitty's heads simultaneously as she talked, while they rolled around in ecstasy.

"Just remember three things, Sam." Jerry spoke with heavy undertones of warning in his voice.

"What three things should I remember, Jerry?"

"One, always follow the money. Two, things may not be what they seem on the surface. And three, take care of yourself, Red. By the way, when are you coming back for a visit?"

"When we settle in, find time for a break, and solve the case," Sam laughed.

"Well, we'll be glad to see you both. You're welcome any time. We miss you," Jerry said, fatherly pride making his voice even rougher. "And remember to watch your back. I'm not there to do it for ya. But I'm only a phone call away."

"Thanks Jerry. I'll remember that, and you may get a call…any time-day or night?" Sam smiled into the phone.

"Well, try to call before 10:00 p.m., if possible. Love ya, Red," Jerry whispered gruffly into the phone.

Sam clicked off and moved over to the couch, followed by the cats. She sat for a few minutes just letting her thoughts go where they wanted. She wondered if the killer would strike again while they were gone. That was her greatest fear.

The connections in the case seemed tenuous, at best. Two departments were involved. One a classically based core area filled with people unlikely to commit murder. A second is more scientifically based, and therefore attracting more money. The answer had to be there. But why would someone murder an up-and-coming scientist whom everyone seemed to like? It just didn't make sense.

Was the killer a serial murderer? Was the killer someone who didn't want the research done that Professor McIntyre was involved in? Would a religious fanatic commit murder? That Sam didn't doubt. It certainly had happened before, particularly in the case of abortion clinics. People who seemed to be paragons of virtue, who in fact proclaimed that they were saving lives, murdered doctors who in fact were themselves actually saving lives. Sam shook her head in wonderment of human nature. *I've got to lighten up,* she thought.

The next hour was spent going through her closet and drawers, putting together a travel bag for the next three days. Sam couldn't help but be excited. She looked forward to seeing her friends in *Heartthrob*. Terry and Nicole had become very dear to her. She already missed Ian terribly. This was the first time they had been apart.

The phone rang. It was Janey McIntyre. "Sam, you'll never guess what? I found two connections to the University of Minnesota," Janey said, a little out of breath. "You must be psychic or something!"

Sam's stomach lurched. It wasn't the first time she had picked a fact out of nowhere. She looked skyward. She was never quite sure what the answers of the universe were, but she believed in synchronicity. *Time to rock 'n roll,* she thought to herself.

"What did you find out, Janey?" Sam pulled out a notebook and pen, ready to scribble notes.

"Sam, you were right," Janey exclaimed excitedly. "You're a genius! I never would have thought of that connection. Anyway, we have two faculty with ties to the University of Minnesota…three, actually."

Sam's heart sank. "Don't tell me, the Ethics pair, Litchfield and Jacobs?"

"How did you know that?" It was Janey's turn to be dumbfounded. "The other connection is tenuous. One of the Bioethics visiting professors also has ties there…and at several other universities."

"What's his name?" Sam grabbed for her laptop and brought up Microsoft Word.

"His name is Helmut Gunn," Janey answered.

"Sounds like an unholy trio," Sam said. "Okay, I'll check things out while I'm up there and see if there's been any incident." Sam typed the three names into her laptop with some notes and saved the information. The hunt was on, she could feel it.

Chapter 20

Sam's van was full to the brim with luggage, two coolers with Pepsi, Diet Pepsi, 7-Up and mineral water, plus yogurt, cheese, bananas, and some chocolate. "One has to always be prepared for the unexpected...first rule of detective work," Sam grinned over at Anni.

Anni answered by popping another piece of chocolate into her mouth. "Yum...I think I could go for a change of careers...this is a lot more fun than fighting the bureaucracy every day."

"I think I'm a bad influence," Sam laughed.

"So, do you think we'll find anything out about our murderer in the Twin Cities?" Anni asked, changing the subject.

Sam mulled over Anni's question. It was certainly a long shot. "We'll have to visit the University of Minnesota and maybe talk to some staff. That is, IF they will talk to us."

"We can do that tomorrow while the band is recording," Anni suggested. "I do want to listen for a while, but maybe if we go right away in the morning, we'll find some staff person there who might talk to us. I've talked to my counterpart there a few times. Her name is Kathy DiGeorgio."

"You have, huh? That might prove to be very useful, indeed," Sam almost rubbed her hands together in glee. She shot a smiled over at her cousin. "I'm already glad I brought you along. We'll have to make some time for fun, though. Like V.I Warshawski says, 'Rule #1, Follow the money; Rule #2, Reward yourself when you've done something brilliant.' I think we just fulfilled Rule #2."

Anni giggled. "Well, let's hope so. I'm sure we could find an ice cream shop somewhere close to the University of Minnesota...after we've hit their office."

* * * * *

Ian blew his breath out in a sigh of relief when he saw Sam and Anni walk through the door of the recording studio. "You made it!" He gave Sam a big hug and Anni a smaller but heartfelt hug.

"Of course we made it!" Sam winked at Anni. It's just a long drive on the same road from Madison until you hit the Cities. The last hour really made my back hurt, though. And staying in the correct lane is always a challenge once one hits the metro area. I'm glad we're here. How soon before we can go get something to eat?"

Nicole came over and gave Sam a hug. Anni stuck out her hand by way of greeting: "Hi, I'm Anni, Sam's cousin from Madison...reporting for duty. Do you need anyone to play tambourine besides Ian? I've never been in a recording studio before. This is way cool."

"I think I'm going to like her!" Nicole exclaimed. "We certainly love Sam...she's a genius! She helped us out of a very tight spot when the timing was crucial for the future of the band." Nicole gave Sam a warm smile which Sam returned.

"Hey, Sam," Nicole's husband and the leader of *Heartthrob*, Terry, came up and gave Sam her second hug. "Good to see ya, kid. Now maybe we can get some real work out of that fella of yours."

Anni was dazzled by the band. Nicole and Terry were both blond, although Nicole was several inches shorter than Terry. Terry had chocolate brown eyes and a muscular build. Nicole had bright blue eyes to match her blond hair, with a dimple on each side of her easy smile. The couple was, Anni thought, simply stunning.

"Let me introduce you to the rest of the band," Terry laughed, as band members sidled up to say hello to the new arrivals. "You already know Ian, of course. That leaves Jake Ross, our inimitable drummer, and his sidekick, Rick Hunter." Rick grinned through his long sandy hair and freckles. Jake was tall, lanky, and wore the black framed glasses Buddy Holly made popular. He wore his hair in a 1950's style to complete the picture. Anni felt like she stepped back in time.

"Pleased to meet you," she said, extending her hand for a firm shake to each band member. "I can't wait to hear you play live!"

"Well," Nicole laughed, "studio work is a little different from hearing the band play live. We record individual parts in the studio and then mix it down. So what you will hear is us singing along with tracks that have already been laid down. It might be boring for you!"

"Oh, I don't think so," Anni said enthusiastically, looking around at the wood and glass rooms of the studio. "I don't think anything about the next few days will be routine at all!" She hugged herself excitedly. "This is so great!"

"Well, if you'll excuse us," Terry broke in, "time is money when it comes to a recording studio. Good luck with your hunt." He looked over to where Ian was nuzzling Sam. "Come on, lover boy, let's get back to work."

The band resumed their vocals, and Sam and Anni listened to song tracks for the next couple of hours. They worked on a song that Nicole had written and was singing lead on, entitled "Strike the Dawn." It was a love song about separation and how the wife didn't want the dawn to come, because she knew her husband had to leave.

Nicole was on the "hot seat" in a small room designed for recording vocal tracks, with wood floors and walls. A pair of headphones sat on her ears, making her look like a refugee from the Mickey Mouse Club.

Her eyes squinted as she concentrated on a well worn notebook used for writing her lyrics that she had sitting on an old black music stand. She hit a bad note and cringed. "I'm sorry…oooohhh, that was a sour one! Let me try it again." A second attempt smoothed out the vocal, and she beamed at the engineer when he gave her a thumbs up.

Anni's eyes gleamed with excitement as she listened. She'd never been even remotely close to the band business and loved being a spectator.

Sam finally looked at her watch as Ian walked up to them with a can of pop in his hand. "I think we'd better get rolling here, if we're going to catch the administrator at the U of Minnesota."

Ian gave a big fake sigh and rolled his eyes. "Oh, all right. I guess we can survive without you two for a while. Be careful now, eh?" He gave Sam a close look to make sure she knew he was kidding.

Sam gave Ian her usual look of mock indignation. "I think we can take care of ourselves. We're just going to the University to do some digging. It shouldn't be a big problem. Anni here has a friend at the University, and we thought we might interview her to find out if there is any connection with Madison."

"Stop by when you are finished," Nicole said. "We'll go somewhere great for dinner. So don't stuff yourselves too much!"

"How about Chinese, there's a place located in the Highland area of St. Paul," Sam suggested.

"Sounds good to us," Nicole replied. "Don't be too long now! We'll be famished by the time the session is finished. Stop by here after you're finished at the University."

"Now, on to the detecting," Sam said, as she and Anni got into her van and headed down I-94 towards the campus.

"Do you think we'll find anything?" Anni asked Sam. This was the part of detective work she didn't understand, but she felt thrilled to watch her cousin at work.

Anni knew of Sam's reputation, of her uncanny ability to pair intuition with scientific method to solve her cases. Sam was awesome.

"I hope so," Sam's brows knit together and her blue eyes took on a steely look. "I just have a funny feeling that we might find out something here. The Twin Cities hold some magic for me, I must admit."

Anni leaned back in her seat and hoped that Sam was right.

Chapter 21

Located on the banks of the Mississippi river, the University of Minnesota is nestled close to the downtown area boasting a beautiful skyline and the Metrodome, where the Minnesota Vikings and Twins (affectionately referred to as the Twinkies when their scores dropped below winning) play.

Known as one of the cleanest cities, Minneapolis is part of an economically robust area that features several intra-city lakes and a lovely old residential area. There is more parkland in Minneapolis than most cities, so Sam and Anni watched the passing landscape with interest.

"I always love returning to my old stomping grounds," Sam commented. "It really is a lovely city, and of course we have to go to the Mall again!"

The Department of Philosophy at the University of Minnesota is located in Heller Hall on the campus west bank. Occupying the seventh and eighth floors, Philosophy's home resides in one of two towers of light brick, Heller being the shorter of the two.

The department is very similar to the University of Wisconsin. The main office of Philosophy is decorated with gay colors, thanks to the creative efforts of its staff. The office also houses a collection of inanimate dogs, frogs, lizards, turtles, and the departmental mascot…a large stuffed rooster to welcome visitors and create an aura.

Kathy DiGiorgio was staring out her window, which sported a panoramic view of downtown Minneapolis, trying to figure out how to balance an account of a professor who had overspent his funds when Sam and Anni walked in. She looked up to see two attractive women, one a tall redhead, and one a shorter blonde. She recognized Anni's voice from telephone conversations they'd had in the past.

"You must be Anni!" Kathy gave Anni a warm smile. She and Anni shared many interests, including politics and a love of music. She was extremely curious about the purpose of their visit, as Anni had alluded to the murder.

"Guilty as charged. Now I'm even starting to sound like a detective." Anni turned to Sam and proudly introduced her to Kathy. "This is my cousin, Sam, who is the famous detective in our family. Sam gave Anni a wink as she held out her hand to shake Kathy's.

"Pleased to meet you," Sam said, sizing Kathy up as she shook her hand. She saw a woman of medium height and weight with sparkling brown eyes and beautiful long brown hair tied back in a ponytail. Kathy had a pair of jeans and a gauzy shirt of a rich purple color which hung gracefully from her slender frame. A pair of matching earrings completed her ensemble. She also sported a light tan from a recent week spent in Tucson, Arizona.

"I'm just back from vacation, so you were lucky to catch me," Kathy commented, looking curiously at Sam. "Now, how can I help you?"

"My friend Ian and I are conducting an investigation into the murder of Rob McIntyre at the University of Wisconsin," Sam began. "We are looking into faculty connections, and since we are up here with Ian's band, *Heartthrob*, for a few days, I thought I could check into any connections between the faculty in Wisconsin and Minnesota. My main question is, are there any faculty here who have ties to the University of Wisconsin that might ring a bell with you?"

Kathy listened to Sam's question with wide eyes, and then narrowed her eyes in concentration as she paused to think. "We have a fairly large unit here, but I can think of two or three faculty who have either had visiting appointments in Wisconsin or who have had visiting appointments at both Wisconsin and our area."

Anni and Sam exchanged looks.

Sam returned her gaze to Kathy. "It might not be connected, but can you tell me which faculty members?"

"Let's see. There's Helmut Gunn. He's from Germany, I think. The epitome of the Hitler youth...6'2", blond, square jaw, laser blue eyes. He is a cold fish, but he is also a ladies' man. He is brilliant, of course. But there's something weird about him that I've never been able to put my finger on."

Sam had her laptop open and furiously typed in notes as Kathy spoke. "Okay, are there any others?"

Kathy scrunched up her face as she thought. "Oh, and there's a married couple. I can't think of their names at the moment, Litchy and Jacobson...something like that."

"Let me guess," Anni broke in. "It isn't Phyllis Litchfield and Tom Jacobs, is it?"

Kathy's eyes opened in surprise. "Oh, so you've crossed paths with the elite power couple too," she commented wryly. "Now there's a couple who might have murder on their minds. They are as nasty a couple as I have run across. Everyone here is terrified of them. At least we aren't stuck with them permanently."

Anni look crestfallen. "Yes, I'm have that dubious honor, I guess. They challenge my diplomacy skills, and my patience, constantly." She made a wry face.

"Could you give me more specifics?" Sam asked. "What kind of habits they have? What kind of enemies do they have, that sort of thing."

Anni grimaced. "They are the couple from hell. They were hired on what's called a 'spousal hire.' That means that the University wanted to hire one of the people, in this case Tom. He's an International expert in his field. But as a bargaining chip, he also wanted his significant other hired. It's done all the time. Sometimes the UW gets lucky and gets two for the price of one. Sometimes it's a disaster..." her voice trailed off and she looked miserable.

"And in this case," Kathy finished for her. "It was an unmitigated disaster."

"Well, any time someone is successful, the money and fame accompany it. Some people handle it well; others don't. In this case, Tom was an okay guy. But Phyllis is like a wicked stepmother. She is riding Tom's coattails and treats everyone she thinks isn't in her league like cow manure."

"Okay, I get the picture. Now...do you think this Phyllis would be capable of murder? And what would be her connection with Rob McIntyre?" Sam brought the conversation back to the investigation at hand.

"Oh, Professor Litchfield hated Rob McIntyre. He was a rising star in the very field her sweetheart was in. In fact, some of Professor McIntyre's research would have superceded Professor Jacobs'. So there was a lot of tension there. As to your question of murder, I haven't the foggiest notion who would be capable and who wouldn't." Anni finished her speech feeling helpless. She looked at Sam for reassurance.

"That was the gossip around here," Kathy chimed in. "I don't have to work with these people and Anni does, so I can be a little more brutally honest. That woman is a witch. She has a gift for making everyone miserable. Would she be capable of murder? My vote would be yes. My impression of her was that she would stop at nothing to get what she wants. There is a lot of money associated with research. If one person's research makes another's life work obsolete, it could be worth millions, depending on the field."

"I would like to talk to any faculty who might have worked with any of these three," Sam said, finishing her notes. "Is there anyone on campus we could talk to?"

Kathy thought for a moment before replying. "Professor Stanley Washington might be available. He knows all three, so he would be the best person to consult."

"Could you check to see if he is available to talk to us for a few minutes?" Sam asked.

Kathy nodded and dialed Professor Washington's extension while they waited. "Professor Washington? Could you spare a few minutes of your time to help with a murder investigation?"

Chapter 22

Professor Stanley Washington fit the expression: "A scholar, possessing nothing of this world's goods, is unto God" in an uncanny fashion. He was only 5'6", but could reduce the younger, taller, and more ambitious faculty, with a single fierce look. He had stringy, grey hair which wandered around his balding head, usually in clumps. But his piercing blue eyes were brilliant indigo orbs which missed nothing, and could dance in merriment or flash with distain.

"And how can I help you ladies today?" Professor Washington inquired with a small smile. He enjoyed the sight before him…three beautiful women who were interested in his time was an unheard of treat. He gave himself a little hug in anticipation.

"Professor Washington, it is so kind of you to give us some time out of your busy schedule." Sam took the initiative, holding her hand out for Professor Washington to shake. He gave another little smile, as he thought of the more gallant form of greeting women…kissing the hand. He refrained when he saw Sam's look. This was a woman with a mission in mind.

"Not at all," he answered truthfully. "Now, what's this I hear about a murder and what is your part in this scenario?"

"I'm a private investigator, and a former homicide detective from the Cleveland police department," Sam answered, to establish her credentials. "I'm here investigating the murder of Professor Rob McIntyre of the Department of Philosophy at the University of Wisconsin. This is my cousin, Anni, who also happens to be the administrator in Philosophy at Wisconsin. She's been assisting me in my investigation. We are here to get some background information on some faculty members from Wisconsin who also have ties to your department."

Professor Washington frowned at Sam's words. In his academic world he had never come upon a homicide detective, and the idea that people peripherally involved in his academic area as being suspects was not one he relished. He thought of one of his favorite quotes from Confucius: "People make mistakes according to their individual type. When you observe their errors, you can tell if people are humane." (4:7). His stomach gave a threatening lurch. Something was definitely odd.

"There are three people who I personally know who also have connections to the University of Wisconsin," he began uneasily. He didn't know how he could help, but he wanted to help these two women, whom he saw had courage and determination.

"Phyllis Litchfield, Tom Jacobs, and Helmut Gunn," Sam said, watching carefully for the professor's reaction. "I understand that Professors Litchfield and Jacobs are married, and that Professor Gunn has had temporary assignments at both the University of Wisconsin and Minnesota."

Professor Washington gave a start at the mention of the three names. "I don't like to say anything against any colleagues, but those three are an unholy trio," he began.

"Do they work together?" Sam asked as her breath quickened.

"No, I don't think so. It's just the personalities that I am lumping together. Phyllis and Tom are married, of course, and are quite the 'power and glory' couple. They are quite ruthless, of course. Helmut Gunn is a handsome and cultivated German. He is quite the ladies' man, from what I understand. I don't know too much about him, other than the fact that he is quite prolific in his writing and is considered to be a real genius. He can also be curt and demanding."

"What, if anything, would be their connection to Rob McIntyre?" Sam asked.

The professor gave a deep sigh as he tried to establish any possible associations between the three. "Well, they are all in the field of ethics," he began. He laughed a little at that thought. These three were most unethical, in his opinion.

Sam noted the corners of his mouth turning up in a half smile, but his eyes conveyed his dismay. She continued to peer at the professor in fascination while she waited for his next comment. He had something to offer, she thought. She didn't want to push him, but tingled with anticipation. These were the moments that made for great detective work.

"If you mean, could any of the three have murdered Rob, I wouldn't rule out any of them," he finally said carefully. "They are all ruthless people who would stop at nothing to get what they want. We have had several incidents," his voice trailed off.

"Did anything happen of a violent nature?" Sam pressed on, sure that there was something to be wrought out of the poor man.

Professor Washington looked down and brushed a stray hair off of his trousers. It belonged to his cat, Socrates, who had purred contentedly on his lap that morning while he worked at the computer. He gave another wry smile, thinking what the philosopher himself would say in this situation.

"Nothing overt happened. But one can tell about people, don't you think? While I don't want to condemn anyone, I have my own code of ethics that governs my behavior. That's why I went into Philosophy. There are others who go into academia for the money. Those three definitely fit into that category."

"What makes you say that?" Sam pushed just a little harder and held her breath. She wished the man would be more specific.

Professor Washington scratched the back of his head as he thought over her latest question. He sighed. Murder was, in his book, one of the most odious crimes against humanity. He wanted to help; politics be damned.

He looked up at Sam, who was taller than him and again marveled at her beauty. "Okay," he breathed. He could hear robins singing outside of his open window. He longed for this interview to be over.

"It's the students, you see," he began. "There have been unpleasant episodes. One student almost didn't graduate, because Helmut Gunn refused to give him a grade. It seems that they had an argument over a coed they were both interested in. It became quite unpleasant, and the Chair finally had to step in to resolve the situation. That's not murder, mind you. But it seems there was a fisticuffs involved." He shook his head, "most unprofessional behavior on the part of Dr. Gunn."

"Were the police involved?" Sam wanted to know. If so, there would be a police report.

"Oh no," Professor Washington protested. "We would never bring in the police for such a matter. It wouldn't be good for our reputation. We settled it internally."

Sam shook her head in wonderment. Academics certainly had their own code of behavior. She wondered what else went on that was never reported.

"How about the 'power couple'...Phyllis Litchfield and Tom Jacobs...what did they do?" She peered at the professor sternly, willing him to give her more information.

"Phyllis and Tom are a powerful duo. They have published numerous books and articles and have a world-wide reputation. They are also most unpleasant. They are demanding, verbally abusive, and most faculty members are terrified of them. I'm glad they are not a permanent part of our faculty. Wisconsin has that dubious honor," he said with a small smile. "They have broadsided more than one faculty member in their time. They are quite a tag team. We've had at least one secretary quit because of their behavior. They aren't welcomed by us anymore. That's all I can tell you about them."

Sam took this as a signal that their interview was over. "Thank you for your candor. I really appreciate you taking the time to discuss these difficult issues." She stuck out her hand, which the professor took with a sigh of relief.

"It's been …uh, interesting," he said carefully. "If you have any further questions, please don't hesitate to call. Good luck with your investigation. I had great respect for Professor McIntyre, and I hope you get the bastard or bastards who killed him."

Sam hid a smile. This little guy amazed her with his gentle but bold personality. Academia was indeed an interesting place, she thought.

Chapter 23

"So, what happened at the University of Minnesota Philosophy department?" Nicole demanded, giving Sam a "two eyebrows raised" look.

"Well, nothing and everything, I'd guess you'd say," Sam answered enigmatically. When several eyebrows arched around the table at her response, she stalled for a moment thinking about how much to say.

The band chose an Italian restaurant for dinner…and there were several pizzas, a couple of plates of spaghetti and meatballs and tortellini on the table, along with salads, Italian bread, and cheese bread. The fragrant smell of Italian sauce permeated the upscale restaurant. They were sitting out on a terrace decorated with reddish-brown stones and terra cotta earthenware artistically placed for the greatest effect. Wisteria gracefully climbed up trelliswork, and a number of potted geraniums completed the picture.

Ian sighed with pleasure as he wound another bite of spaghetti around his fork, holding it in place with his spoon. "I'd rather have them interviewing a nice, safe faculty member than the gunman," he asserted.

Sam gave him a thoughtful look. "But what if our murderer IS a faculty member?" She matched Ian's quick look.

"Do you think that's what is going on here?" Ian demanded. He searched Sam's eyes as if to pull the answer from their azure depths. They remained locked in a look as time seemed to stand still. A few discreet coughs brought them back to reality.

Sam pondered her answer. "I feel like I should have more to show for this investigation. It's really frustrating.

No one seems to be able to give me anything concrete to chew on. Not that I like chewing concrete," she laughed.

"What do you know for sure?" Terry piped in. As the band's leader, he had a logical mind that could quickly grasp a problem.

Nicole and Terry were the leaders of *Heartthrob*, and much of their success stemmed from their blond-haired look, Terry's incredible voice, and their common musical expertise. Terry was a natural leader, and he and Ian had a lot of respect and affection for one another.

Sam shot Terry a smile. "Well, we know the murder was probably committed by one person. The motive is unclear, but it could and probably does have something to do with Rob McIntyre's research. The police have eliminated the possibility of marital infidelity. Professor McIntyre has received threats from fundamental religious organizations. But we doubt that the murder was committed by someone like that. This was too professional."

"How about jealous faculty, we've certainly seen some of that," Anni piped in. She bit her lip. She probably had the most to lose of anyone sitting at the table. Her job could be on the line if the murder wasn't solved, or if the murderer turned out to be someone like her boss. She cut off her thoughts before her imagination could further upset her.

"Perhaps," Sam answered, giving her cousin a reassuring smile. "But I feel like we are missing something here. We just need more information." She sat back, twisting her napkin into shreds.

"Sounds like we need to do something fun before heading back to Madison," Nicole suggested. "Sometimes a little recreation is just what the doctor ordered to jumpstart the old brain. How about a visit to the Minneapolis Institute of the Arts? I hear that's a premiere museum."

"I seem to have good luck when the band plays," Sam muttered, more to herself than the others. However, Ian heard her comment and produced a huge belly laugh.

"Perhaps it's just the magic of the band being together," Ian suggested, putting his arm around Sam's chair in a protective gesture. "But for now, I second the idea of going to the museum. I haven't done that in ages."

Sam gave a tight little smile. She loved museums, but felt that she should stay on task. She wasn't going to let herself rest until the murders were solved. She knew Anni counted on her. She was also aware that Anni would lose face at work if she failed. From what she'd seen of academics, losing face was something that a person wanted to avoid at all costs. But she needed the break.

"Okay," she finally relented. "We'll go to the museum. Then it's back to the grindstone for us, huh partners?" She looked around at Ian and Anni for reassurance and got huge grins in return.

"Great!" Terry said. "I'll see how many band members I can pull together for this little excursion. Who knows, maybe we'll find some clues in the museum!"

"Even if we don't we'll have a great time and be able to reconnect in a neutral setting," Nicole added, giving Terry a wink. "Terry and I feel somewhat responsible for this group, as you all know. We'll also do our best to help Sam and Ian solve their murder."

Chapter 24

Sam, Anni, and Nicole stopped in the bathroom of the Minneapolis Institute of the Arts. Established in the late 1800's, the building was designed by McKim, Mead and White and opened in 1915. Kenzo Tange, a Japanese architect, designed the finishing touches of the neoclassical structure. MIA is known for its varied collections including ancient art to modern sculpture and textiles.

At the moment, Anni was more worried about Sam than the ornate surroundings. "Are you all right..." she asked Sam anxiously. Sam's face was a mixture of stormy emotions and furious thought. She looked up in surprise at her cousin's question.

"Yeah, I always go through this sort of thing on a case," she answered softly. "We're right smack in the middle of the investigation. We have some facts, and my brain is working furiously to put them into their proper order. Sort of like Poirot's 'little grey cells' theory. I'm trying to make sense of this case, but there are some major pieces of the puzzle that are missing."

"Do you want to go through some ideas? I can be a good listener," Anni offered.

"I want to help too!" Nicole, having finished her ablutions, joined in the conversation.

Sam gave both women a grin. She felt so fortunate to be around such supportive people. "We just have to keep our eyes open. The best thing you can do to help is let me know of anything you notice that seems odd or out of the ordinary. Anni, you know the people in the department. Nicole, you are an observant student of human nature. Now, let's enjoy this museum experience and return to this later."

She gave them what she hoped was a bright smile and they went to join the others.

After two and a half hours of walking through exhibits, Sam felt like she was on overload. She looked over at Ian, who was peering at an exhibit with a faraway look on his face. She stood watching him for a minute, enjoying his concentration. Their relationship was progressing at a satisfactory pace, she thought to herself.

She and Ian had met when she interviewed him during their last murder case. She was a Cleveland detective who had been called upon to handle the murder of LeMar Ridley, the band's booking agent. Ridley was found murdered in his room, and there seemed to be no end of suspects. Sam had interviewed Ian, who had promptly asked her out, and then showed her his FBI credentials. She had been bowled over by the entire experience, and by him. That seemed a long time ago.

He turned to her just then, sensing her presence. His red hair settled around his chiseled face like a wreath of fire, and his brilliant blue eyes smoldered as he looked at her.

"I think I've had enough of this thoroughly, uh, cultural experience," Ian's voice was low and husky. "It's about time for some 'quiet' time for you and I, don't you think?" He was beside her in an instant, nuzzling into her neck with both arms around her.

She settled into his embrace, enjoying his musky smells. It seemed like forever since they'd been together, and her mind started racing with possibilities.

"You don't have to ask me twice. I'll have to set Anni up with someone in the band. Where's Nicole? I bet they'd enjoy once another. Nicole can tell her about our exploits firsthand. Oh, there they are. And I see they've already found one another."

Nicole and Anni walked up serendipitously. They had been chattering and laughing and seemed to be getting on quite well. Sam wasn't surprised. Anni was just the sort of person the band would enjoy.

Nicole cast an inquiring eye at Sam and Ian. "I think it's time we split up and had some quiet time to ourselves. We'll just have some quick things to finish up in the studio tomorrow morning. Should we just meet there at 10:00 a.m.?"

Ian gave Nicole a grateful grin. "That's just what I was thinking. Could you take charge of Anni for the time being? We'll see you all tomorrow morning."

"Nicole and I were just getting to know each other," Anni said excitedly. "If they'll let me tag along, I'll see the two of you tomorrow. I'm sure I can keep myself occupied. Oh, look at that," she remarked, looking past Sam.

"What is it?" Sam turned and saw a large man with blond hair and an athletic build.

"It's Helmut Gunn," Anni said, staring. "I wonder what he's doing up here. He probably won't acknowledge me...I'm just a peon from the office, so I won't say hello. I didn't know he was interested in art."

"Well," Ian said. "We'll just toddle off now and see you all tomorrow morning at the studio." He took hold of Sam's arm and meaningfully steered her towards the exit of the museum. Once they settled into their van, he gave her a long and lingering kiss.

"That's just a preamble," he said, as he blew into her ear. "I'm going to work you over properly when we get back to the hotel."

"Oh, I was hoping you were going to say that," Sam answered lustily. She kissed him back and then settled back into the seat. "We don't want to cause a traffic accident. Just get us to that hotel in a hurry."

Two hours later Sam and Ian were stretching luxuriously. The sun beat its late afternoon rays into their hotel room, and they could hear outside noises of strangers as they passed by their door joking and laughing.

"So that was Helmut Gunn," Ian murmured, thinking of the man they had run into at the museum. "He's at the top of the list of suspects, or at least near the top...correct?"

"Well, he's in the running," Sam answered, drawing little circles on Ian's chest with her fingers. "Then there is the power couple from Madison. That Gunn person is certainly big enough to have committed the murders. But what is the motive?"

"We need to check on his background. Whoever committed the murders probably has some military service in their background. Those throat slashings were committed by an expert, someone who knew just what to do and who wasn't squeamish."

"A woman would probably resort to either a pistol or poison," Sam added, scratching her head and winding a tendril of her auburn hair around her finger. "I'll have to meet Phyllis Litchfield and Tom Jacobs. If he's a wimpy guy, we can probably rule them out."

"I'll see if some of my buddies from the bureau can help with any priors on either of the two," Ian said thoughtfully. "I think I still have a good enough name around there, although I don't want to be a pest."

"Is Ron Smith still mad at you for leaving the bureau?" Sam asked. She knew that Ian's superior officer hadn't been too pleased when he had decided to take a leave of absence. They both knew that Ian probably wouldn't be back, and Smith had counted on Ian's specialty in drug cases. His cover with the band made him a perfect mole.

"Oh, Ron isn't a bad guy, as F.B.I goes," Ian said in his defense. "There are guys who are much bigger assholes, especially the "up-and-comers." I wouldn't want to trust some of those guys with covering me. They are more interested in building their careers than doing their jobs. Any shortcut to the top is all right with them."

Sam nodded sympathetically. "I suppose that's true in any bureaucracy. I'm glad you are out of there, at least for the time being. It gives us more time to get to know one another. We're doing all right financially for the time being. We'll just have to see how this case goes. I hope we can find the murderer soon. Classes are starting next week, and I don't want to be too torn."

"We'll get whoever did this," Ian said, trying to instill confidence in Sam. He knew she was one of the best detectives he had ever seen, and he had a lot of confidence in his own abilities. He just didn't want to put Sam at risk.

He pulled Sam closer, enjoying her warmth and the feel of her silky skin. She was so beautiful, and he was so in love with her that he never wanted to let go.

"We'll find him--or them," he said again, hoping to convince himself. Their future depended upon it.

Chapter 25

Sam felt rested and invigorated by the next morning, and her sense of optimism returned. The sun streamed through the window of their hotel room with the promise of a new day, and she felt the warmth of late summer, tinged with a subtle shift in the wind which meant that summer was losing its grip.

She sighed and turned to face Ian, who was still sleeping peacefully, a puckish grin settled on his lips, facial muscles relaxed into a serene pose. She was quickly learning every line of his face and the curve of his muscles. This man could be the one, she thought to herself. We seem to match so perfectly.

Just then Ian opened his eyes and his mouth settled into a small smile. "Good morning, mate," he whispered. He threw a proprietary arm around her and she snuggled into his chest.

"Morning yourself," she answered, feeling a little shy, as she still sometimes did when she realized how much she cared for this man. She had a strange sensation of time both slowing down and speeding up at the same time. So much had happened in the past few months, and she had made major changes in her life. It was an eerie feeling.

"So, what's on the agenda for the day?" Sam asked softly, running her fingers through Ian's hair.

"We're almost finished with the recording session," Ian answered thoughtfully. "We can go out for lunch, assuming we're done by then, and then head back to Madison. Then we can plan our next move on the investigation. I'll check in with my FBI friends to see if either of our suspects had military experience. We may have to contact

Europol for that Gunn character. But I want to refocus on our power couple. We haven't explored that area much yet."

"So, maybe we should pay another visit to both departments?" Sam suggested. "We can start from there and see what develops. We still need more information on the Bioethics arena. There might be something there that we've missed."

"Sounds like a plan. I'll be glad to get back...I feel like we've been neglecting the case. But I have to fulfill my commitments with the band. Nicole and Terry are such great people. I don't want to let them down."

* * * * *

When they arrived at the studio, Nicole and Terry were overdubbing harmonies. Both stood side by side with earphones on in the "live" sound booth, which looked like a cavern. They were tapping their feet, had big grins on their faces, and were arguing in an unconvincing manner about who could sing higher. Anni was giggling and clapping as she watched them.

"I think it calls for a woman's voice on top," Nicole gave Terry a pleading look. "Your voice has so much resonance that the lead vocal might be drowned out."

Terry gave Nicole an unabashed grin. He was extremely conscious of the fact that his powerful vocals drove the band. Rick Hunter, *Heartthrob's* bass player was giving his best friend, drummer Jake Ross, a high-five. Rick's sandy hair was stuffed into a *Heartthrob* baseball cap. Jake Ross wore jeans and a nylon basketball shirt with the Wisconsin logo on it. They both gave the thumbs up to Terry, letting him know that they thought Nicole's idea should prevail.

Nicole blew the boys a kiss as the door of the studio opened. Alex Jones' tall and muscular frame stood in the doorway, a huge white grin ablaze amidst black locks.

"Heard you guys were conducting a recording session; thought I might stop by to lend a hand...maybe on some harmonies or something...perhaps an extra guitar lick?" He flashed a brand new guitar case towards them and bounced eyebrows at Nicole and Terry in a questioning manner.

Terry was the first to react. "Alex, my man, it's great to see you! Of course we'd welcome any input you might have. We would have called you but thought the wedding plans might be keeping you busy."

Alex gave them a little smile. "Which wedding are you referring to?" He asked. He heard a gasp go through the band. During the Ridley murder case he had proposed to his girlfriend, Helen Jackson. Helen was a nurse with long brown hair and stunning green eyes. Helen and Alex had gone through some tough times when Alex's band, *Blinding Dawn* had run into legal problems. Nicole and Terry asked him on stage one night, and he had joined their tour.

The marriage the band was focusing on was that of Patty Boyd and Robert Pierce, who ran a booking agency in Minneapolis. Robert and Alex were cousins. This was the secret behind Alex's present grin.

"We're making it a double wedding. We figured that since it has already gotten out of hand with *Heartthrob* as the featured entertainment..."

Nicole squealed. Terry thumped Alex on the shoulder. Alex almost dropped his guitar. Jake's long legs beat Rick's to Alex's side.

"Well, well," Rick murmured as he shook Alex's hand. "There is certain symmetry in all of this, or should I say synchronicity."

Nicole's eyes got a little misty, and she dabbed them secretly so no one would notice. She had a heart of gold and loved happy endings. She, of any of the band members, probably understood Alex's happiness. She and Terry had spent years struggling to position the band and guarantee their success.

"Well," she said, sniffing quickly, "I'd say we have a little more work to do. I know that Ian and Sam would like to get back to Madison. So let's have Ian lay down his tracks so they can get out of here in a jiffy."

Ian shot Nicole a grateful look and again marveled at how much he cared for this band. He stepped into the sound booth where his conga drum was set up and laid down a track with drums and quickly overdubbed a harmonica part.

Terry and Nicole stood in the sound booth dancing as Ian set down his parts. The existing tracks sprang to life with Ian's touches. When he finished and stepped out of the booth, they clapped enthusiastically.

"Great, Ian! That's just what the song needed. I think we can take it from here, if you, Sam, and Anni want to take off. Thanks so much for coming out, and we'll be in touch."

"Yeah, we'll have to learn some wedding songs, from the sounds of it," Ian quipped.

Nicole giggled. They all had extensive wedding experience under their belts. It wouldn't be a problem.

Chapter 26

Sam, Ian, and Anni found a homey little restaurant in the Highland area of St. Paul for lunch. From there they could hop on the Interstate back to Madison. The drive was only about five hours, so they felt they could relax a little over their salads.

Ian found the delicious meal restored him both mentally and physically. Recording was grueling enough, but then having to put on the hat of a private eye drained him, although he was enjoying both professions.

"A double wedding," Sam murmured, almost to herself. "I can't wait! I'll get to hear you play in a more intimate setting, and I'll be able to go out and splurge on a sexy dress. What could be more fun?"

This comment brought several images to Ian's mind, and he choked on the piece of broccoli he was eating. He hastily took a sip of the ice tea and hit his nose on the lemon slice sitting on top. This elicited a huge giggle from Sam, as Ian wiped his nose with his napkin in as dignified a manner as he could muster.

"Could you find a dress with Velcro?" He asked Sam innocently, figuring that he would have an easier time getting her out of it when the time came.

"All right you two…it's getting hot in here," Anni said facetiously, pretending to fan herself.

"Oh, don't worry Sweetie. I'm sure I can find something that will fit the bill." Sam assured Ian. "Now, perhaps we should turn our attention back to this case." She shot him a mock stern look.

"You're right. Business before pleasure," Ian said, pulling himself away from the delicious images he had so enjoyed just a moment before. He would make Sam pay for that particular tease.

"We won't be able to do any 'visiting' today, but we can make some phone calls tonight. I think we should check in with Janey McIntyre, to make sure she is all right. Then maybe we can call Detective Drake, to see if the police have turned anything up. Then perhaps we can visit the Chair of Philosophy again…perhaps press him about our suspects."

"Sounds like a plan to me," Ian agreed.

Anni nodded in agreement. This was getting even more interesting.

* * * * *

"Oh, I'm so glad you are back!" Janey exclaimed when they put in the call to her later that night. "All hell is breaking loose around here!"

"What's going on?" Sam asked, keeping her voice low and businesslike. She could feel Janey's tension jumping through the telephone lines, and she felt a little guilty about leaving town.

"We had a break-in at the house," Janey said. "I don't think anything was taken, but the place is a mess."

"Didn't you have someone watching the house?" Sam demanded, her voice and temper rising. Ian raised his eyebrows curiously at Sam, and, seeing her face turn red, joined her by the phone.

"We had a mix-up with the coverage. The guy who was supposed to be here called in sick. I thought it would be all right, but I guess someone must be watching us closely," Janey said bravely, her voice turning raspy.

"We'll be right over," Sam said, looking at Ian, who gave a definitive nod. "Just sit tight."

Janey began to sob as she opened her door to Sam and Ian. Sam put her arms around her and just let her cry, until she emptied all of the pain and frustration of the past couple of weeks. Ian stood by helplessly, wishing he could place his hands on the neck of the perpetrator and apply steady pressure. He gritted his teeth and took a deep breath. Janey needed them now, and he was determined to solve this case. He shot a look at Sam, who tried to smile reassuringly over Janey's head, which was buried in her shoulder. She took a deep breath to get her own emotions under control.

"So, let's take a look inside," Sam suggested cautiously, when she thought Janey had composed herself enough to take them through the house.

"I really didn't need this," Janey gave a little nervous laugh, which sounded a little like a muffled sob, as she opened the door. Tables were overturned, cushions ripped off of the couch. Papers and books were everywhere. It looked a little like a five year old's temper tantrum.

"As far as I can tell, nothing's been taken," Janey declared, ruefully surveying the damage. "I'll have to straighten things up before I can tell for sure. The police have been here and dusted for fingerprints, but they weren't very optimistic." Her pretty face took on the frown of a school teacher who had just caught a recidivistic student in a prank. She heaved a huge sigh, wiped her tears, and turned to Sam and Ian.

"You guys just get the jerk who did this. I don't know if they are trying to scare me, but I'm no longer afraid. I'm just pissed now. If it takes all my money, I don't care. We're going to catch this bastard."

Sam once again opened her arms, and Janey willingly went to her. She then turned to Ian, who gave her a strong and steady hug, trying to impart as much of his strength to her as he could. He set his lips into a firm line, as he considered what their next move would be.

"I think it's time to go visit to the good Detective Joel Drake. He might have something to clarify this situation."

"Agreed," Sam assented, nodded her head sagely. "It's time we get serious. This is beginning to tick me off."

Janey walked over and sat down on her couch, with Sam and Ian sitting across from her in comfortable chairs. She took a deep breath to compose herself, and gave them a shaky smile and a nod.

Sam pulled out her cell phone and punched in Joel Drake's number. She talked to the receptionist for a few minutes, ended the call, and turned to Ian and Janey.

"Turn on the television," she directed. "Joel is just about to start a press conference. We probably won't learn anything specific, but we should be able to tell how the investigation is going by what he says."

"This should be interesting," Ian muttered as Janey hastily grabbed the remote and flicked the television on to the most popular local television news channel. Sure enough, Detective Joel Drake was standing at a podium preparing to give a speech regarding the case.

Janey, Sam, and Ian looked at each other and hastily found seats. Their course of action would be determined by what Joel had to say, and they wondered if he would send them any signals as to how he wanted them to conduct themselves. One thing was clear...the case was becoming more complicated by the minute.

As they were waiting for Joel to begin the press conference, Sam tore open the envelope she had hastily taken out of their mailbox on the way over to Janey's house. It contained the autopsy report on Rob McIntyre.

She stepped into the bathroom to look at the report. There were also a few pictures taken at the crime scene, which showed Rob McIntyre laying in a fetal position. The report was about three pages long, illustrated with diagrams that the prosector, the pathologist in charge of the actual autopsy, drew of the body.

The results of the autopsy did little to enlighten her. Rob McIntyre had no blood clots, but had a large cut in the larynx, which detached the larynx and esophagus from the pharynx. His heart was in excellent shape, and he had the body of a much younger man. His liver was healthy and showed no signs of abuse from drugs. The toxicology tests agreed with those findings.

Sam read the rest of the autopsy report and slowly replaced the report and pictures back into the envelope. Rob McIntyre was a clean cut man who loved his family and didn't deserve to die in a criminally violent manner. She bent her head for a few minutes, and when she once again composed herself she opened the door to rejoin the others.

Chapter 27

Detective Joel Drake cleared his throat, pulled at the tie that clenched at his neck. His 6'6" linebacker build towered over the officers and news people who stood around him. He gave them a reassuring grin, and his dazzling smile comforted those around him. He cleared his throat to signal the beginning of the proceedings.

"Good afternoon. We've called this news conference to give you an update on the investigation into the murder of Professor Rob McIntyre and Marie Cavendish. First, we would like to reassure the community that the Madison Police are doing everything we can. We have many officers working on this case. We are also consulting with two private detectives with excellent homicide records and FBI experience. We have called upon the FBI and are presently in touch with Europol. We have several leads we are working on, and we expect to close in on the killer in very short order. The Madison Police Department prides itself on its high percentage of murder cases that are solved. We will give you the next progress report in a few days.

Having delivered the somber speech, Detective Drake paused to catch his breath. He hadn't had much sleep since the case began, and he was anxiously waiting for word from Sam and Ian. They needed all the help they could get on this case, and he had confidence that Sam and Ian could obtain certain information through indirect channels that the police could not uncover through official channels. He shifted his stance and prepared to take questions from the swarm of reporters buzzing around.

He signaled to a reporter from the Wisconsin State Journal. He was a man of medium height in his forties with a slight paunch, thick dark hair, and an inquisitive expression in his brown eyes.

"Detective Drake, could you tell us if you have any significant leads on this killer? The community is being terrorized, and we don't want the University bureaucracy to cover anything up. Do you think it could be another professor committing these crimes?"

Drake took a deep breath. These were just the type of questions he was dreading, but knew he would have to face squarely.

"That is an excellent question. We are well aware of the community's concern, and I can assure you that everything that is humanly possible is being done to apprehend this killer. As for the identity of the killer, I can't give you any specific information at this time. If I could, that killer would be behind bars, I can assure you." Drake gave the reporter a beatific smile, hoping that he had headed off a possible human relations disaster.

Several hands immediately went into the air as the remaining reporters shouted their questions. Detective Drake took another deep breath and pointed at a reporter on the opposite side of the room.

"Detective Drake, have you collected any significant DNA evidence that would help identify the killer?"

"Another intelligent question," Drake smiled. "There's no fooling you guys. But to answer your question, there wasn't the type of DNA evidence one would expect if the victims had struggled with their attacker. These murders were committed by someone with knowledge of how to carry out a scientific murder, if there is such a thing."

The crowd of reporters erupted with questions when they grasped the significance of Drake's statement.

"Do you mean we have a professor who is also a professional killer?" One reporter gasped.

Drake inclined his head, "I sure hope not. But we have to consider all alternatives. One thing I will promise you, my friends, whoever committed these atrocities will be caught and punished to the full extent of the law. We have one of the finest police forces in the country, and our law school provides us with the best personnel in the district attorney's office. We WILL not screw this up. That is my final word on the matter. We will be happy to take any calls from the public if anyone has seen anything suspicious."

With that, Drake left the podium as more hands waved frantically in the air. Finally, the remaining reporters decided that the press conference was over and pulled out their cell phones en masse to report on the latest news. The Capital Times and Wisconsin State Journal, although owned by the same company, shared a lively competition with each other, as well as with the more stylish Isthmus.

Janey walked over to turn off the television set, her mouth set in a thin line. She turned thoughtful eyes to Sam and Ian, who were digesting what they had heard. Sam walked over and put an arm around Janey.

"Don't worry...we'll get this guy. Are you all right?" She pulled off a Kleenex from an end table and handed it to Janey, who furiously dabbed at her eyes. Janey took a deep breath, squared her shoulders, and nodded.

"I know you will. I have complete confidence in you. What is your next step?"

"Back to the University," Ian said ominously.

Chapter 28

Detective Joel Drake got back to his office and began issuing orders. Phones were ringing in the overstuffed office, desks piled with papers and empty pop cans. He walked into his cubicle and shut the door, letting out his breath in a deep sigh. This case was becoming a huge hassle, and he was afraid someone else was going to be killed if they didn't come up with something soon. He wondered if his career was on the line, and at the same time chided himself for being selfish. There was a murderer loose in his beloved city of Madison, and he was not going to rest until they had the perpetrator in their sights.

He bellowed a "What?!" when a soft knock on the door interrupted his small bout of self pity. He looked up to see Sam and Ian coming through the threshold.

"We've both been there before," Sam said lightly, giving him a reassuring smile. The room seemed to light up, and Drake grinned in spite of himself.

"Well, well, if it isn't the fabulous duo, come to rescue me from the depths of despair, no doubt," he laughed, even as his mood began to lighten. "Please tell me that you've brought something substantial…I could use some help here!" He scrutinized them with a question in his eyes.

"Maybe, probably," Sam said shortly. "We just have to put the pieces of the puzzle together. I know the answer is there…but I think we have the suspects narrowed down. We need your help in tracking alibis."

"That I can provide," Drake said, pulling out the file. "What have you got for me?"

"We interviewed a professor at the University of Minnesota while Ian was there recording," Sam said. "The same pattern keeps recurring."

Drake said nothing, just kept peering at Sam. He was reminding her more and more of her boss, Jerry Malone, who she missed terribly. *I understand why Anni is so fond of this guy. He really cares about what he's doing.* She found it so refreshing, and yet so like her situation at the Cleveland Homicide Division.

"We'd like to check alibis for a couple of professors from Philosophy here in Madison," Sam began, opening up her laptop. "We figure that you've already talked with many of the professors," she gave Joel a look over her reading glasses. "That is, of course, if you've talked to them all."

"Who do you have in mind?" Joel said finally, playing with his pen.

"Professors Phyllis Litchfield and Tom Jacobs, for starters," Sam said. "Helmut Gunn is another suspect. He visits various universities, apparently," Sam replied eagerly.

"Do you have anything specific on them?" He gave Ian a hard look. "You're not holding out on me, are you? Because if you are, I'll have your licenses pulled."

"We don't have anything concrete yet," Ian retorted, his eyebrows leading his face into a scowl. "We're asking what you have, if anything. Can we eliminate any of the three? Perhaps they are working together...who knows? But we can't give you anything if you're not willing to talk to us."

For a minute the two men stared at each other, waiting for the first one to break contact. Sam fidgeted and then decided to break in.

"Okay guys, enough of the male power games. We've got a murderer to catch. Now, Detective Joel, could you please answer our simple question?"

Joel gave a sigh. "In fact, none of the three has an airtight alibi. We've kept surveillance on all three, but so far we've come up with nothing."

"How about Professor Fred Canon, could he be a suspect?" Sam asked, figuring that she already knew the answer. They hadn't found out much on their stakeout, but she felt sure that Professor Canon wasn't the murdering type. He might have an arsenal of swords and other weapons, but he struck her as a science fiction/fantasy fan with too much money and not enough hobbies.

"He's got an alibi. He was with his girlfriend, a..." Joel shuffled his papers in the file, "I know it's here someplace, dammit. Oh, here it is. A Professor Susan Hilger vouched for his whereabouts...he was at her place for the night. Another departmental couple," Joel smiled.

"Okay," Sam said, writing her own notes into her laptop. "By the way, did you ever find any usable fingerprints off of the letter we brought in from Bioethics?" She gave Joel a cursory glance.

"Nada," Joel sighed. "All we found were smears. And, of course, there were Betty Brown's prints. Probably fifty people handled that envelope. The paper used was a common cotton bond that one can buy in any stationery store. The letter was typed on a pc. That's it for now."

"One more question," Sam said, as she typed furiously into her laptop. "Are the three suspects you're scrutinizing left or right-handed?"

"Good question," Joel commented, making notes on a pad. "We'll get right on that and get back to you. What is your next move?"

"I think it's time to revisit Descartes' Den," Sam said, giving Ian a steady look. "Maybe we can shake things up a little."

"Okay. But, please, don't do anything to put Anni in danger. She is one of my best friends, and I would take it as a personal affront if anything happened to her."

Sam finished her notes and logged off of her laptop. She felt like she and Ian were going back into a danger zone. Joel's last comment shook her up. It was one thing to carry on a murder investigation. It was quite another thing to put one's relatives in the line of fire.

"I think it's time for Anni for take a few more days off," Ian said quietly, reading Sam's thoughts. "We don't want her in any danger, and if we start asking questions, a few people might start getting nervous."

"I'll call her right away," Sam said. She pulled out her cell phone and dialed Anni's work number. Anni picked up on the second ring, sounding a little winded.

"Department of Philosophy, this is Anni," she said cordially into the phone.

"Anni, this is Sam. I hate to ask this of you, but do you think you could take a few days off of work? We're going in to question some people, and I don't want you to be in the line of fire, if you know what I mean."

Chapter 29

Having opted for Italian, Sam and Ian sat with a large pizza with veggies and shrimp on top. Ian took several swallows of a glass of import beer, relishing the hearty taste. Sam sipped a glass of white zinfandel, and took a large bite of cheese bread.

"You've definitely been a challenge to my waistline," she laughed, taking another bite of pizza. "We're going to have to go jogging to wear this off."

"Jogging? I had other ideas," Ian said, cocking an eyebrow. "We've been working pretty hard, between recording and chasing murderers."

"Hmmm, I see what you mean," Sam said, distracted by the look in Ian's eye. "A little recreation might do us good…then we can go jogging. It'll clear our heads."

They continued eating in silence, duty and thoughts of the murderer still at large casting a pall over the dinner. Ian studied Sam as she ate her pizza. He was amazed at her resourcefulness and resilience. Murder investigations took a terrible toll on the police, in terms of shattered relationships, and, often, alcohol abuse. Sam didn't manifest any of these cracks in her personality. Again he marveled at this astonishing woman and felt very lucky that their paths had crossed.

"Tomorrow should be an interesting day," he commented quietly, giving Sam a chance to vent her feelings.

"Yup," Sam said shortly. She had been eating a salad, and put her fork down. "I don't want Anni to be in the middle of any crisis," she said, suddenly serious. "I could bear anything but that. We have to protect her."

"Don't worry, we will," Ian assured Sam. He had an idea of what she was going through. He had lost more than one friend when he was in the FBI, and he knew the helpless feeling when one sees a person they care about in danger or killed.

Ian felt a flash of outrage. In a way, anger was what had drawn him into law enforcement to begin with. His sister had been brutally raped, and Ian had never forgotten the sheer rage that he had felt. Both he and his sister had ended up in law enforcement. She was still on the West Coast, and was a Los Angeles cop. That was no easy job, but Ian admired her determination and felt a close kinship with her.

Sam looked up to see sympathy in Ian's eyes, and then angst. He looked at her silently, unable to express his closely guarded secret. Someday he would tell her about all this, but not now. For now they had a job to do, and steely determination replaced the vulnerability. He gave her a tight smile, and she wondered at the transformation.

"Ah, my love," she said softly, sensing that what Ian needed now was her own affection. "I don't know what force brought us together, but I do know that we will get through this. We will solve this case, and we will protect both Anni and Mrs. McIntyre. We just have to."

"After this is all over, I will spend a great deal of time apologizing for now being more forthcoming," Ian replied, watching Sam's beautiful features. "Just know this...I do love you. I love you more than anything or anyone on this earth. Together we'll solve this case."

Chapter 30

Phyllis Litchfield was tall and lanky, standing at almost six feet without shoes. She had longish kinky permed brown hair, which was dull and brittle. It framed her nondescript face, and her plastic blue octagonal eyeglasses made her look like a secretary. Her temperament was what made her imposing. She had a steel will with which she blasted everyone around her.

Tom Jacobs had grown up in the same neighborhood with Phyllis in San Diego. He had loved her at first sight, which happened around age ten when his family had moved next to hers. Tom was a skinny child with a powerful brain. He had managed to outwit the bullies, but gained a formidable ally in Phyllis. They had spent virtually every moment together since the fateful day when Tom's parents had chosen the small wood frame house in a residential neighborhood. They too had noted Tom's small size and had chosen an environment where he could thrive.

Phyllis and Tom went through Stanford on scholarships, having both graduated at the top of their class. The California lifestyle had influenced their personalities at the time, as well as a little experimentation with pot and alcohol. They married immediately after college, and stayed at Stanford for graduate school.

Tom had eventually caught up with Phyllis in height, but as is the case with underweight children, had made up for lost time. He weighed 230 pounds, and cut an imposing figure. Together, he and Phyllis felt invincible, and their personalities reflected this newfound power. As a result, most people were scared silly of them.

A frown creased Phyllis' rather plain face as she opened to door to find Sam and Ian standing there. She particularly hated good looking, hip people who made her feel inferior. She set her face in its most cruel lines, hoping to deter them.

"What is the meaning of this? Who are you? Do you have an appointment to see us? This is outrageous," she sputtered.

Sam gave Phyllis a reassuring smile. "Professor Litchfield? We are investigating the death of Rob McIntyre for his wife. We were wondering if you could answer some questions. It won't take but a few minutes."

Phyllis gave Sam a hard stare, hoping to ward her off, like a curse. Her hair splayed out in every direction like Medusa. Her pale blue eyes blazed with indignation.

"I don't see what possible relevance this has to us," she seethed. "You are barking up the wrong tree if you think we had anything at all to do with this." She finished her sentence with a little hiss, reinforcing the mythic picture.

Sam took a deep breath to fortify herself. "We are questioning many people and would appreciate your cooperation. We have no power to force you to talk to us, but if you refuse, we'll have no choice but to report it to the homicide detective in charge of this case."

Phyllis gave a little sniff. "Oh yes, I heard something on the news about the two of you. Well, let me tell you something. We weren't even in town when the murder took place. We had nothing to do with it. We didn't socialize with Professor McIntyre. Now, is there anything else?"

She made a move to close the door. Ian placed his foot in the door to block her move and gave her a disarming smile. He decided to jump into the conversation.

"Professor Litchfield, I'm sure you can sympathize with our point-of-view. There is a murderer loose out there, and he has chosen your department to victimize. Even if, as you state, you had nothing to do with the murder, your cooperation could save the life of one of your colleagues. Now, please, just give us a few minutes of your valuable time." Ian then gave her his sexiest smile.

Phyllis thawed a little in spite of herself. "Well, perhaps a few minutes more," she muttered more to herself than to them. "But we are both very busy. You might as well come in and sit down. I would rather not have my colleagues see me talking to you in the hallway."

"Thank you, God," Sam muttered under her breath with her head averted. She turned to Professor Litchfield and gave her a bright smile as they stepped in to her office and settled into two uncomfortable looking chairs. Phyllis settled herself behind a standard Badger State Industry wooden desk and ergonomic mesh-backed chair.

"Now, you say you were out of town the morning of the murders?" Sam began, pulling out her laptop and powering up.

"Well, actually we were at a conference the day before and came home very late that night. We were in town, but we were in our beds fast asleep when the murder occurred," Phyllis answered, shifting uncomfortably.

"May I ask where the conference was held?" Ian asked, giving Sam a significant look.

"In Minneapolis, at the University of Minnesota," Phyllis answered. Just then Tom Jacobs walked into her office.

"Phyllis, what's on for lunch," he stopped as he saw Sam and Ian. "I know who you two are," he sputtered, face turning beet red. "What are you doing talking to my wife? How dare you!"

"It's all right, honey," Phyllis jumped in quickly, giving her husband a warning glance. "They are investigating Rob McIntyre's death. Tom, this is Sam Peters and Ian

Temple. They are working for Mrs. McIntyre. We can answer a few of their questions."

Jacobs' brow darkened at the mention of the murder. "We had nothing to do with it!" He exploded. "Why are you questioning us? Are we suspects? Do we need a lawyer?"

Sam took over once again. "We are simply questioning you because you work in a similar area to Professor McIntyre. We have already talked with many people in the areas involved." She gave Tom a sweet, reassuring smile that she didn't feel.

"Oh, all right. But if you accuse us of anything, you'll be hearing from our lawyer," Tom bellowed.

Pointedly ignoring him, Ian turned back to Phyllis. "Do you have any ideas of who may have committed this murder? Have you noticed anything suspicious, like anyone suddenly changing their routine?"

Phyllis looked over at her husband. They seemed to be silently communicating. She suddenly looked miserable and shook her head.

"We don't know anything, and frankly, we're scared to death. The idea that someone here might be a murderer is most demoralizing for us. As you know, we are always struggling for position in comparison to other universities. This murder has created a terrible scandal for the department, as well as the University in general. We just want it solved. We want to return to the way things were before this unfortunate incident." She gave a deep sigh.

"This business is most upsetting," Tom chimed in. "Frankly, we're surprised that the investigation is taking this long. I mean, isn't that what you people do?"

Sam stiffened as if she'd been slapped. Ian looked over at Sam and unconsciously clenched his fists. He sucked in his breath and reminded himself to stay calm.

"We're doing everything we can, Sir," he said mildly, holding his emotions in check. He peered at Tom Jacobs. He looked like the sort of person who was used to getting his way. People like Tom Jacobs made Ian very uncomfortable. He knew Professor Jacobs was probably brilliant, but the arrogance that could accompany his position was hard to take. But Ian was confident enough not to be cowed.

"I should think so," Jacobs went on, warming to his attack. "We are part of an austere group, and this situation is untenable. I certainly hope you people know what you are doing. There has already been enough damage."

Sam started. That was certainly one of the weirdest pissing contests she could remember. She stifled a laugh, remembering the setting.

"Thanks so much for your time," she said hastily, grabbing hold of Ian's sleeve. "We really appreciate you taking time out of your busy schedule to talk to us."

Once they were safely in the hallway Ian let out a slow breath to allow his temper time to cool off. He wasn't used to anyone challenging him, and the idea that a professor had just dressed him down as if he was a five year old child made him boil.

"It's a good thing you got me out of there," he told Sam through clenched lips. I was about ready to deck that guy. It probably wouldn't have been too difficult, but then we would lose our private eye licenses."

Sam giggled, and then grabbed Ian's hand, figuring that some tactile encouragement was in order. "Boy, what a jerk. I take it that the illustrious couple is still on our list of suspects? They certainly didn't say or do anything to remove my own personal suspicions."

Ian relaxed at Sam's touch. He gave her hand a gentle squeeze and grinned. "That guy had me going, but it just increases my suspicions. They could possibly be our murderers. They were certainly nasty enough to be killers.

How can anyone attack someone they don't even know who is only trying to help?"

Sam nodded. "That's just the point. If I was a murderer, I would go on offense if questioned. That's the best way to divert suspicion. It automatically puts those around the person on defense."

"Well, then, it's time for us to do a little interference," Ian said. "How do you feel about doing a little surveillance later tonight?"

"What do you have in mind?"

"We'll begin with the terrible twosome's residence and see where it all leads us," Ian said with a sort of smug satisfaction. "I have the feeling the answers are very close."

Chapter 31

"Whew! Would you look at that," Ian marveled, eyes bulging as he took in the residence that Phyllis Litchfield and Tom Jacobs occupied. "No doubt they have inherited money from somewhere, or they are dealing drugs. We should check it out."

"I already have," Sam said absently. "It appears that Phyllis Litchfield inherited quite a tidy sum. She was an only child of a doting father. Her mother died when she was seven. She was brought up by a series of live-in nannies after she succeeded in preventing her father from marrying again. Tom Jacobs also comes from some money, but nothing compared to Phyllis. They grew up next door to each other and have been together since childhood."

"It's a good gig if you can get it," Ian replied, then catching Sam's questioning look said, "I'm kidding! You know I'm a Renaissance man! I make my own money. I don't rely on family to run my life."

"Thank God for that," Sam breathed. "There's nothing worse than families who try to run the lives of their children. It screws them up for life, and they most never accomplish a thing."

They turned their attention back to the house, which was a brick colonial set back one hundred feet from the winding road. Pillars and a sweeping veranda gave the house a stuffy look, but the beautifully manicured lawn gave the place lushness. The house was a two story, with five bedrooms and a sunroom built off of the side.

Two hours passed very slowly before they saw a grey Lexus pull into the driveway. The figures of Jacobs and Litchfield emerged, and it appeared that they were having a heated argument.

Sam and Ian opened the window to try to catch the gist of the dispute. As it turned out, they were yelling at each other so loud they probably could have heard the sound through their closed windows.

"You are such an idiot!" Phyllis was screaming at her husband. "You almost blew it for us! Why did you have to be so rude to those detectives? They are probably suspicious of us now."

"Well, we aren't the murderers," Tom bellowed. Then he thought to look around, in case some of the neighbors were out in their lawns. Seeing no one about, he resumed his invective. "Besides, the cops don't care about a little pot."

"Things are different now," Phyllis screamed back at him. "We have a lot to lose if you get caught for 'just a little pot.' Why don't you understand that? Can't you find some other vice that would be a little less threatening to us?"

Tom's cheeks grew redder. "Oh, shut up, Phyllis. You've always tried to tell me what to do and how to run my life. If I want to smoke a little dope, I'm going to. You can't tell me not to!" His voice whined as his fury increased.

Phyllis didn't deign to make another remark. Instead she launched herself into the house and slammed the door. Tom stared at her retreating figure, his face a mix of fear and rage. He turned on his heel and returned to the car, screeching the ignition as he yanked the key in the crank. He squealed out of the driveway, tires leaving the signature tread marks.

Sam peeked over at Ian from their hiding place, only to find him grinning from ear to ear. "Well," she said haughtily, "I guess she told him." Ian gave her a quizzical look and they both erupted.

"We probably shouldn't be laughing," Ian remarked after a few minutes. "Perhaps they could lead us to a bigger fish, as they say."

"Do you think we ought to follow him?" She asked rhetorically as Ian started up the car to follow. "Not that I want to talk to that guy again."

"It might present us with a sliver of a lead, but probably not," Ian replied, as he strained to catch up with Tom Jacob's retreating Lexus.

Twenty minutes later, Jacob's car pulled up in front of a small brick apartment complex. Located on the far west side of Madison, the building was upscale, intended for young, rising professionals. Tom was buzzed in to the locked building and disappeared.

Sam and Ian settled in to wait. Sam pulled out her cell phone to call Detective Joel Drake. "Joel? This is Sam, as in Sam and Ian. Yeah. We're doing a little bit of a stakeout, and we wondered if you could identify the resident of this apartment. Let's see, it's 2195 Gold Street."

"Sam!" Joel bellowed into the phone, once again reminding her of her old boss Jerry Malone. "You're what...a stakeout, huh? Well, it'll take me a few minutes to answer your question. Can I reach you on your cell phone? Let's see, I have the number here somewhere." Sam could hear Joel shuffling papers on his desk. "I've just gotta clean up this space one of these days. Ah, here it is. Just you two sit tight, and I'll get back to you."

Chapter 32

Sam and Ian waited for about an hour, and Sam's cell phone played Beethoven's *Für Eli*se. She flipped it open and stabbed at the "on" button. "This is Sam," she said absently as she kept her eyes on the apartment building.

"Sam, it's Joel again. We've identified the resident of 2195 Gold Street. It's rented to a Professor Helmut Gunn. He is a visiting professor from Bonn, Germany. He is definitely a person of interest in this investigation. We have a call in to Europol to check him for any priors. Now, remember, I want a call before you do anything. I'll permit you to stake out his place, but that's it. Do you understand?"

Sam sighed. She was used to being given orders, but she wasn't used to being on a leash. However, Joel Drake had been very helpful and had given them tacit approval for their activities.

"This is merely a stakeout, Detective Drake. We don't intend to take any action. We are simply trying to establish a connection between the two suspects. At this point we don't know if there is anything other than a friendship or a professional collaboration. We followed Professor Jacobs here after he argued with his wife."

Sam heard Joel Drake's intake of breath when she neglected to use his first name. She didn't want to alienate him and couldn't afford to destroy the working relationship they had. But she also wanted to remind him that she was an experienced detective and not a loose civilian running around playing private eye.

"Point taken, Sam," Joel Drake was quick to catch her meaning. We do appreciate what you are doing and want to keep this relationship warm and professional. Carry on with what you are doing and report back to me. I realize we are not paying your salary, but you do need to keep me informed of your movements from this point onward. Is that satisfactory?"

"Very much so," Sam said. "I didn't mean to be offensive; I was just trying to justify our actions. We will keep you apprised of any new developments. I feel there is something here, but we just haven't nailed it down yet."

"I'll get back to you once I hear from Europol, but it may take a while," Joel replied. "In the meantime, see what you can find out. I trust your instincts, particularly based on your record. I took the liberty of putting a call into your old boss, Jerry Malone. He seems to think highly of both you and Ian, although he said he had his doubts about Ian at first, since he is a rock 'n' roll star. But he said you two are a good team and to give you a chance."

Sam smiled over at Ian, who raised his brows and asked her a question with his eyes. She shrugged back at him and felt a small jolt of electricity run through her body.

"Well, thanks for the vote of confidence," she said smoothly into the phone. "We'll be sure to let you know what we find out." She clicked her phone and snapped it shut, a look of satisfaction crossing her features.

"What?" Ian asked, not sure how to take the mixed messages. "What did he say?"

"He's going to check out Professor Helmut Gunn. He probably isn't related to this case at all. Perhaps we are just seeing a marriage spat with the husband fleeing to a buddy's place for comfort."

She felt a small surge of depression wash over her like a gentle but malevolent wave. The case was beginning to get to her. What were they doing here anyway? She didn't know what they could hope to find out. She looked over at Ian, a frown playing around her mouth.

"Are we accomplishing anything here? We've established that there is a connection between Professor Jacobs and Professor Gunn. What else do we really know?" Ian sensed Sam's frustration. "Why don't we give it another hour, and if nothing happens, call it a day?" He caught hold of a strand of Sam's copper hair and wound it around his fingers, all the while holding her gaze.

Sam felt herself falling under Ian's spell and reveled in the moment. She touched a finger to his nose and carried it down to his lips. She gave his lips a small caress and whispered, "Okay, an hour then."

Almost an hour later, the wind suddenly whipped through the trees that surrounded the apartment building. The temperature dropped dramatically and clouds suddenly tore through the heavens like watercolors running through a canvas. Sam gave an involuntary shudder and turned to Ian.

"I think we're finished here for the time being, but next on the list should be a visit to Professor Helmut Gunn. In the meantime, I'm hungry and...what's on for tonight?"

Ian cracked up. This woman was constantly surprising him when he least expected it. The idea of a hot meal followed by a night of love was something he was not going to turn down. He pulled Sam to him and gave her a gentle kiss that grew in intensity. Sam melted into him and they lost the outside world for a few minutes.

Chapter 33

The next day Sam woke up earlier than Ian. Crisp fall air flowed into their bedroom mixed with dust particles illuminated by the sun. The temperature was already sitting at sixty-five degrees, with the promise of soaring into the seventies. It would be a gorgeous day.

Sam got up, gathered her pink terrycloth robe around her, gave the tie a firm yank around her waist, and stuffed her feet into comfortable leather slippers. She padded downstairs and poured water into the coffeemaker. She sat down at the kitchen table and stared at some hummingbirds feeding on the nectar she had made a few days before. She and Ian had a small back yard which boasted a birdbath, some feeders with weighted bars, and a hummingbird feeder situated next to impatiens, late-summer pansies, and geraniums. She could barely see the industrial-speed wings moving on the delicate birds, and marveled that something so small could accomplish so much.

Thoughts of the murder intruded upon her early morning musings. She decided to make some notes, and went in search of her laptop. She felt the need to organize her thoughts, particularly before conducting more interviews.

She opened her laptop and waited for it to power up, sipping coffee and trying to clear cobwebs from her still drowsy brain. Finally, the computer finished its internal permutations and waited for her to begin typing.

She decided to begin with a few questions. First and foremost, what type of person would murder Rob McIntyre and Marie Cavendish? After creating a table, she wrote the phrase "Murderer Characteristics" in her first column and began to think. She wrote "Left-handed." She stopped and thought for a minutes. "Possible military training?" came next. Under that column she wrote "Probably a male, or if female, a very large woman capable of overpowering from behind, a runner." That's obvious, she thought.

Under her next column, she wrote "Motive." She decided this column would bear more thought, but immediately wrote "Professional jealousy." Thinking for a few more minutes, she wrote "Drugs?" Underneath that entry, she wrote "Possible corporate invention which may have destroyed existing research and/or investments by other faculty." She gave her head a scratch. That one was iffy.

The next column was titled: "Opportunity." She wrote in Phyllis Litchfield and Tom Jacobs. Under that she added, "Check out exact time of talks at meetings." Under their names she wrote, "Possible religious individual opposed to bioethics research?" She gave her head a shake.

She stopped her entries and took another sip of coffee. Ian came up behind her and planted a kiss on her cheek. She grabbed hold of his arm and gave it a squeeze.

"You're up early? Are you an insomniac and haven't let me in on the secret?" She turned and smiled, then grew serious.

"I'm just trying to organize my thoughts a little here. I feel like there is something we're missing. We need to go back to Hume's Hutch and interview more people." She gave him a wan smile.

"I'm ready," Ian said, as he turned away and began pulling pans out of the cupboards. "But first I'm going to make us a wonderful breakfast. Would you prefer an omelet sweetie? I'll even throw some veggies in. How would you feel about mushrooms, green peppers, and onions?" Ian gave Sam a knowing wink.

That was the first time Ian had called Sam by anything other than "Red." She enjoyed the endearment for its newness for a moment, then smacked her lips. "You don't have to ask me twice. Then we can get ready and make another assault on the venerable Palace of Plato."

Ian groaned. "Really bad alliteration; can't you come up with something better?" Sam gave him a grin and went off to take a shower and dress.

Two hours later Sam and Ian walked into the department. Anni was sitting at her desk frowning at payroll sheets, as she compared them with appointment forms. A grin crossed her features as she looked up to see Sam and Ian striding into her office.

"Hey guys! I'm back on the job, as you can see. There's no one else who knows how to do payroll, so duty calls. No one has bothered me, so I guess that's a good sign."

"Have you seen Helmut Gunn today?" Sam asked, knowing from conversations with Anni that the faculty members were often at home doing research or writing.

"Yes, actually, he was just in checking his mailbox about ten minutes ago," Anni answered. "Do you want me to ring him up for you?"

"No, thanks," Sam said quickly. "I think we'd like to use a stealth approach. We might get more answers that way. Just sit tight and we'll be back later."

She and Ian found the correct room number and saw Helmut Gunn sitting at his regulation black state desk with a "cobalt blue" executive padded chair. He was leaning back as far as the chair would go and cast his Icelandic blue eyes in their direction as they knocked on the open door.

"Yes? What is it? Can I help you with something?" He gave Sam a friendly smile until he noticed Ian standing behind her. His smile turned into a frown as he took in Ian's physique appraisingly.

"Professor Gunn, I am Sam Peters and this is my partner, Ian Fleming. We are here to ask you a few questions regarding the murder of Professor Rob McIntyre."

"Oh yes, a most unfortunate occurrence," Helmut Gunn remarked, shaking his head. "This is very bad for the philosophers here."

"I see that Professor McIntyre's office is next door to yours," Sam said, noticing the nameplate as she looked to her left. You must have had some sort of friendship with Professor McIntyre. What can you tell us about him?"

"He was a very nice person," Helmut Gunn said in his German accent. "His loss affects everyone. He was a family man who was totally honest…almost to a fault."

"Do you have any idea why someone would want to kill him? In an academic environment, this is a very unusual occurrence. We see many murders in poorer parts of town. We see murders in families. We even see murders in corporations. But a university murder is not so common."

Helmut's eyes widened. "Who knows, perhaps for money or some sort of jealousy. There are many reasons why people kill…or so I've heard. I'm a big Agatha Christie fan myself." He gave a little smile.

Sam cocked her head as she considered Dr. Gunn's answers. He didn't seem to be too upset about Rob McIntyre's passing, but after all he was only a visiting faculty member. As a short term professor, there was no need to cultivate anything other than professional contacts, which was different than day-to-day relationships with peers that permanent faculty members were expected to build.

"I see," she began. "But what we would like to know is did you see anything that struck you as suspicious before Dr. McIntyre's murder? Did he have any arguments that you heard? Did he seem upset about anything? Did anything happen that seemed a bit odd or out of place?"

Helmut tapped his pen as he thought for a few minutes. Finally he looked at Sam engagingly and shook his head.

"No, there was nothing. I just don't understand why anyone would want to murder that poor man. He certainly didn't do anything obvious that would lead one to conclude that he should be murdered. It is most perplexing." He shook his head and gave her another smile.

Ian decided to join in. He took a step forward and planted himself in front of Helmut Gunn's desk so that he couldn't be ignored. Helmut looked up at Ian with a small smile of challenge. That gave Ian the entrance he needed.

"I can hardly believe that you didn't see anything," he began. "Murder is a very serious business, Dr. Gunn. I want you to know that anyone who was even remotely close to Dr. McIntyre is under suspicion. Your cooperation would be greatly appreciated."

Helmut's face registered surprise, and then a flash of anger. "Are you accusing me of something Mr., eh, Temple? If you are trying to put the blame on me for this murder, you'd better be very sure of your facts. I annoy easily."

Ian blinked at the veiled threat, but didn't back down. "That is our job, Dr. Gunn. We are very good at it, I might add. We are simply asking for any information you might have related to this murder. We can see that you are very busy, so we will save any additional questions for a later time. In the meantime, please take our card. We would like you to call us if you think of anything."

Helmut Gunn took the card and threw it on his desk indifferently. He gave both Sam and Ian a hard look, and then leaned back in his chair with his elbows resting on the arm rest and his hands pushed together in the prayer position.

"Oh, I will. I'm quite sure there is nothing that I have to add to your investigation. I am truly sorry that Dr. McIntyre had to die, for whatever reason. However, these things happen. I wish you luck in finding the murderer. And now I must return to my research. My time in Madison will pass by quickly, and there is much I have to accomplish. Good day." He extended a beckoning arm to the door to make his point, but Sam and Ian had already risen to leave.

"Thank you very much for your time, Dr. Gunn. Please try to remember whatever conversations you had with Rob McIntyre just before his death. If you do recall anything that might be of interest, please give us a call."

Helmut Gunn mustered a smile, but said nothing more. Sam and Ian left quickly so that they could discuss this very strange meeting.

"Well, what do you think?" Sam asked, after they had left the building. "What is our next move, and what were your impressions of the veritable Dr. Gunn?"

Ian gave a little snort. "Actually, I think he was lying through his teeth. In fact, it seems to be a habit with the last couple of interviews. Offhand, I'd say they're all guilty. Do you think that's possible?"

Chapter 34

A coffee break seemed to be in order. They needed to regroup and figure out their next move. They didn't want to go to Memorial Union, because they were afraid someone may overhear their conversation. Instead they headed down State Street and found a deli style restaurant.

Sam groaned as they slid into a booth and placed their order. Thoughts of the murder gave her another headache, and she reached inside of her purse for some Advil. She swallowed a couple, followed by a big gulp of coffee. She had to catch the headache quick before it erupted into a cacophony smashing around in her head.

Ian watched her closely. He was worried about the stress of the murder. Sam had already begun classes, and he knew the demands of her academic schedule would clash with the investigation. He knew they were close. They just had to put it all together.

"So, who is your vote for most likely to have committed the murder?" He gave Sam a reassuring smile and tried not to grit his teeth and let her know how nervous he was.

"Well, I still think it had to be one of the men. I don't picture Phyllis Litchfield as a "slit your throat" kind of gal. She would be more likely to use poison. Have we missed any other possible suspects, or are we simply focusing in on our two faculty buddies?"

"Why would a visiting scholar have a motive for killing a professor here?" Ian said, scratching his head. "This whole case doesn't make sense to me. There's got to be another element. As for my vote, I want to know more about these two guys. For one thing, did you notice if either is left-handed?" His blue eyes twinkled as he locked them on Sam's.

"They both are," Sam said shortly. "So, that puts them on the top of the list of suspects. We still have to 'sift and winnow.' I saw that phrase somewhere on campus. I think it meant scholarly research, but we're doing police research. So, where do we go from here?"

"We need to question more of the faculty, if they'll let us," Ian said firmly. "We simply have to keep pounding this until we come up with some sort of solid motive. Then we can find the evidence. Speaking of which, perhaps a call to Detective Drake would be in order?"

Sam pulled out her cell phone. After a short conversation, she grunted and snapped her phone shut.

"Well, is anything happening on that end?" Ian asked impatiently. "Did they ever make a connection on the clothing swatch you found at the scene?"

Sam sighed. "Yes, but nothing that will help us. The fabric is a polyester blend that is commonly used. There is nothing to help us there. We're going to have to dig deeper on this. I just know the answer is in front of us. But we need a little help."

Ian looked thoughtfully at Sam. He had the feeling they were close to their murderer. The answer seemed to be just outside of their grasp. It was a frustrating situation. None of the evidence was helping.

"Have the police turned up anything new on the murder weapon?"

"I think that if we figure out who the murderer is, we'll be able to lay our hands on the weapon. But in order to find the murderer, we have to figure out the motive. Lots of people had the opportunity…the entire world, in fact."

"Let's go back and hang out in Anni's office for a little while," Ian suggested. "Maybe we'll overhear some conversation that might help us."

* * * * *

Anni looked up from disorderly piles strewn around her desk as Sam and Ian sauntered casually into her office. Anything was a welcome relief from the numbers she was crunching. She gave them a brilliant smile.

"Well, well, my favorite sleuths. Have you come to rescue me? I have time for a little break."

"Hi Anni," Sam answered. "No, we're just hoping we can sit in your office for a little while and observe the department. We thought we might hear something out of the ordinary." She gave her cousin a hopeful glance.

"I've seen Fred Canon. Would you like to talk to him?" Anni picked up her phone and held it poised in the air while she waited for their nod. She punched in the number of Professor Canon's office.

Fred Canon answered and readily agreed to the interview. "I owe them an apology for refusing to talk to the female detective at my home. I guess I just panicked," he told Annie ruefully. "Anyway, I'll talk to them now."

Sam and Ian made their way to his office. He had the door slightly ajar waiting for any students, as it was officially his office hour for the week. He beckoned them in, hastily clearing two older yellow padded chairs and indicating that they should sit down.

Sam made herself comfortable and surveyed Fred Canon with interest. Up close he looked like a medium-aged, mild-mannered scholar. He was about 5'8" inches tall, with medium brown hair that was thinning at the top. He wore blue jeans and a light blue oxford shirt. His feet were

145

stuffed into running shoes, and his expression was fixed upon Sam with a slight smile and a gleam in his eye.

"Well, first, let me say that I'm terribly sorry that Rob McIntyre was murdered," Fred began. "He was a nice guy and a family man and didn't deserve what happened to him. It's such a shame, and it's scaring the rest of us. I have to personally apologize to you, Ms. Peters. I was too scared to talk to you when you rang my doorbell. I know it was cowardly. I hope you'll accept my apologies. Now, what is it I can help you with?"

"Don't mention it," Sam said, feeling a little embarrassed. I understand that your area of expertise is Ethics, just as Rob's was. Can you tell us anything about your relationship with him?" Sam asked, hoping to gloss over the awkward moment.

Fred gave a nervous laugh. "Well, Rob was quite a star. I must admit that I was a little worried when he came. But Ethics is a big area, and there is plenty of room for different viewpoints. He was no real threat to me."

"I see," Ian remarked, leaning forward to peer at Fred Canon. "Perhaps you knew him well enough to notice any enemies he might have had?" Ian narrowed his eyes, checking Fred's body language.

Fred thought for a few moments and fidgeted under Ian's stare. He felt quite intimidated by Ian, but he wouldn't allow it to show.

"Um, do you mean do I have any pet theories on who might be responsible? Of course you have probably heard about our 'power couple' in the department. But do I believe they may have committed the murder? To what end? I've have thought this over myself, and it makes absolutely no sense. Rob wasn't a wealthy man, although he probably would have ended up rich, as he was on a 'golden' path. Did I suffer from jealously? I respected him, but wasn't really threatened. I am simply happy to be able to pursue my research. You'll find that most of our faculty members share that sentiment. So, I don't know what to tell you."

"Do you have any sharp knives in your antique collection?" Ian pressed. "And, if you do, are you missing any of those weapons?"

Fred looked uncomfortable. "Yes, I have an extensive collection of antique weapons. I have many swords. You see, I am a sword and sorcery fan. I don't think anything is missing, but I'll check, if you like. Or, you could come to my home and inspect my weapons for yourselves. I have nothing to hide."

"Do you have any surgical knives?" Ian again asked.

Suddenly Fred's eyes opened wide. "I have two. Perhaps we should make a trip over to my home. I'm not sure I remember seeing them the last time I looked. Oh dear. You don't think that someone could have…?"

"Anything is possible," Sam said. "Perhaps I should make a call to Detective Drake. This may be a development that the police aren't aware of. Tell me, who would have had access to your home?"

Fred suddenly looked miserable. "I don't lock my house," he admitted, his head hanging. "I just never thought that it was necessary. Oh, sure, Madison has burglaries, but if someone wanted to get into my house, they would get in regardless of whether the door was locked. I always figured that if I left the door open, an intruder would be less likely to cause damage."

Sam and Ian exchanged looks. Sam hastily punched in the number for Joel Drake and asked him to meet them at Fred Canon's home.

* * * * *

"Oh my God, oh my God," Fred Canon kept saying as he wrung his hands. Joel Drake was directing crime scene investigators to dust Canon's weapons room for fingerprints. Upon entering Canon's home, Fred had made a dash for his knife case. There was one knife missing.

"Do you remember when you saw it last?" Sam asked Fred again gently. Fred sat in his brown Lazy Boy sofa with perspiration beading on his forehead. He felt like he was going to throw up. The idea that one of his prized antique knives was used in a murder was almost more than he could bear. He kept shaking his head as if he was having a bad dream and could wake up if only he tried hard enough.

"I don't remember," he wailed. "I had a small faculty get together here a few weeks ago, and it could have disappeared on that day. I've been so busy with a research paper that I haven't spent much time with my weapons in the past few weeks. Oh shit! You've got to help! I could pay you!" His tear-filled eyes looked at Sam beseechingly.

"Take a deep breath," Sam said, patting Fred on the head. Fred's girlfriend, Susan Hilger arrived and immediately went over to Fred. They clasped hands, and she gave Fred a reassuring smile. Fred introduced her to Sam and Ian. Susan was average looking, but had a great smile.

"Well, it looks like this murder is just not going to go away," Susan murmured, eyes troubled. "We just never thought it would land on Fred's doorstep. You must believe that he had nothing to do with this terrible thing. Fred is the sweetest, kindest man I have ever met. He could never have even contemplated such a thing. He was with me the night before the murder, and we had breakfast together." She blushed in spite of herself. "We have tried to keep our relationship quiet, but I guess that our little secret will now have to come out."

"We will do what we can to protect your confidentiality," Sam said. "Everyone is a suspect, though, until this murder is solved. We are asking you to stay in town. If you need to leave for any reason, we want to know about it right away."

Fred and Susan cast miserable eyes on Sam and Ian. They glumly watched the proceedings, as technicians dusted everything in the room for fingerprints.

An hour later, Sam and Ian walked back to their car. They were quiet, as each thought of the latest developments in the case.

"I don't think either Fred Canon or Susan Hilger had anything to do with these murders," Sam said, taking Ian's arm for support. "They just don't seem to be the type. I know that we have now probably zeroed in on the murder weapon, although it is missing. But somehow I think they are pawns in this case."

Ian bowed his head in thought as he listened to Sam's words. The missing weapon looked bad for Fred Canon, and he felt sorry for the guy. He shared Sam's perceptions. There was no motive. Also, if Susan Hilger was to be believed, Fred Canon was with her. Or so it seemed.

Chapter 35

Detective Joel Drake wasn't convinced. Sam and Ian sat in his office after being called in for a conference. They slouched in their chairs with glum faces. Fifteen minutes of arguing had produced no results or agreement.

"So, you want more time?" Joel asked. "I'm getting a lot of pressure to close out this case. So far we have what is probably the murder weapon, although it is currently missing. Who is to say that Fred Canon didn't want to eliminate competition? I understand he was in the same subject area as Dr. McIntyre."

Joel's jaw jutted out as he talked, and he clenched his lips. He looked so much like Jerry Malone, Sam's old boss. The effect was so comical that she had the urge to laugh, but she restrained herself, having learned her lesson long ago. Instead she focused on convincing Joel to give them more time.

"There are several leads we would like to check out," she began reasonably. "Could you just give us a couple more days before you bring Canon in for further questioning? We believe that Fred Canon is just an innocent person who is being manipulated by the real killer."

She gave Joel her most pleading look. He stared at her for a few minutes until she blinked and looked down. She glanced over at Ian for support. Ian gave Joel a thoughtful look and remained quiet for a few moments, to give Joel time to process the point they were trying to make. He gave Joel an encouraging smile and reached over to give Sam's hand a squeeze. She threw Ian a grateful look and turned her attention back to Joel, who remained mute. The air was thick with anger and innuendo. Ian flinched first.

"You should listen to Sam," he pointed out. She's got an awfully good track record. I trust her instincts, and I think she is right in this case. What do you say?"

Joel pondered his comments for a few minutes longer. Finally he gave them both a hard look, and then broke into a smile, although his eyes were doubtful.

"I think you're right. I'll try to keep the jackals from my door for two more days. But after that, we're going to have to arrest someone. You'd better work fast...the hourglass is running out. I'm getting heat from my superiors to produce results. And, now, I have some calls to make." He turned from them and pulled the phone off of its cradle. It was a signal that the interview was finished.

"Well, we dodged the bullet on that one, so to speak," Ian commented as they left Drake's office. "What next, Red?" He smiled over at Sam to see how she would take his remark. He had little to fear, as she was well used to that sobriquet. She barely noticed.

"Campus police," she muttered to herself, thoughts spinning wildly. "Maintenance people on campus might have seen something. We need to do more legwork."

An hour later they sat in the office of the University Campus Police. Many officers who work for campus police are former police officers; some have worked homicide.

"We've been scouring the campus for anyone who might know something," Dean Graff told them. Dean was in his mid-forties, was 6'4" with dark hair, brown eyes, and a huge mustache. "So far we've got zilch. Have you talked with the maintenance people? They can seem a little invisible, so maybe they've overheard something. We couldn't get anything out of the English speaking crew. Many of the crew hail from other countries and English is not their first language."

"Is there a night time supervisor available whom we could talk to?" Sam asked.

"Yes, his name is Steve Wyatt," Dean said. "He's a nice guy and is very sharp. I'll look up his number for you." He pulled out a staff directory and mumbled to himself as he navigated through the confusing directory. "Ah, there he is." He wrote down Dean's phone number for them.

They thanked him and left his office. They put through a call to Wyatt and left a message for him to call them back on their cell phone. Heading to campus seemed to be a good idea, so they drove in, found a parking place at the Lake Street parking ramp, and headed for Memorial Union. They bought coffee and headed to the Lakeside Cafeteria to plot their next move.

"So, what do we want to ask this guy?" Ian inquired after taking a large bite out of an apple muffin, relishing its sweet and fruity taste. "Are we grasping for straws here or what? Even if someone heard something, do you think they'd tell their supervisor?"

"You never know," Sam said, biting into a cranberry scone. "Sometimes breaks come from the oddest places. We have to at least give it a shot."

Sam's cell phone chirped, and she quickly punched the "on" button. Ian strained his ears to hear the conversation, which was short. Sam finished the telephone call and looked at Ian meaningfully.

"He'll be here in five minutes. He's across the street at Science Hall," she said with a gleam of triumph in her eye.

Steve Wyatt was medium height and build, with dirty blond hair worn long and wavy and brown eyes. He was dressed in jeans and a pin-stripped blue shirt. His eyes were intelligent, and he had an easy smile. He caught sight of Sam and Ian and strode over to their table after buying himself a cup of coffee.

"You two aren't hard to spot," he said laughing as he grabbed a chair and sat down. "Two redheads with an official air stick out like a sore thumb. You might as well wear uniforms." His eyes twinkled.

Sam found herself warming up to this guy with the serious air and friendly sense of humor. She hesitated a moment, framing her words.

"Thanks for agreeing to see us, Steve. I'm sure you are very busy, so we won't keep you long. As you may or may not know, we are investigating the murder of Professor Rob McIntyre as private investigators."

"Yeah, I know," Steve's eyes were troubled. "I used to see Professor McIntyre quite often when I would come in to check on my employees. He was always cordial and was never rude, which is more than I can say for the new guy who has the office next door."

"Do you mean Professor Helmut Gunn?" Ian bolted upright in his chair.

"Yeah, that guy," Steve said darkly. "There is something sinister about him. I often heard him arguing on his phone…or should I say screaming. What a temper that guy has! I wouldn't want to meet him in a dark alley. And I've seen plenty on this campus, I can tell you. We even have our own resident ghosts!"

Both Sam and Ian shot him a look, to see if he had a manic look in his eye. Ghosts?

Steve caught their glances. "I know it sounds crazy, but we have two ghosts on campus…one is a man who wears one of those 1920's hats, and the other is a woman who hangs around Bascom Hall. She wears a hoop skirt. The UW is about 150 years old, so one can only imagine the stories behind the sightings!"

"Have you ever seen the ghosts yourself?" Sam asked carefully. She was beginning to wonder about the veracity of his claims.

"I think someone wrote a book about it," Steve said casually. "I haven't seen anything myself, but some of my staff have. If you talked to some of the campus police, they've also been privy to the apparitions. We also have a tunnel system on campus that goes under every building. We've had people living in the tunnels for years on end. We have had a number of homeless people who decided to take advantage of the state's largesse and occupy buildings, particularly Helen C. White. They're gone now," he said grimly. "But they gave us no end of trouble." He thought for a moment.

"You might want to check on some of the indigents who hang around campus, unless you've got something else in mind," he looked at them expectantly, hoping they would give him another good story to add to his repertoire.

"Let's get back to the occupants of Helen C. White…er…the faculty and staff. Have you seen or heard anything that makes you think someone would have had a motive to kill Professor McIntyre?" Sam asked, trying to get Wyatt back on topic.

Steve thought for a moment before answering. He felt like an idiot for having gone off on a tangent. They probably thought he was a campus crazy. He had an undergraduate degree in Sociology and was far from a fool. He wrinkled his brow and forced himself to concentrate.

"Perhaps someone heard something they shouldn't have," he said tentatively. "I'm sorry I can't give you anything more concrete than this. And please don't think that I'm a moron. I have a degree from this very institution. Actually, I have a lot of warm and fuzzy feelings for this place. I have a wide circle of friends here, and I enjoy my job. But I promise I will keep my eyes open, and if I hear something that might be helpful, I'll call you."

Steve pulled his card out of a plastic sleeve he kept in his back pocket. He handed it over to Sam with a smile, and she reciprocated by giving him one of their cards.

"Don't worry," she smiled reassuringly at Steve. "We hear all sorts of things in our line of business. We have enjoyed meeting you, and please call if you think of anything or if someone gives you a tip. Thanks again for your time."

Steve stood up. "Now, it's time to get back to work. It's been interesting meeting you. You are making quite a stir on campus, in case you haven't noticed. Good luck in your investigation." He made his way through the crowded tables, giving them a farewell wave.

Sam and Ian watched Steve enter the esplanade in bewilderment. They finally dared to look at each other and shook their heads in amazement.

"That was…weird," Ian managed, trying to hide his mirth. "He did say one important thing, though."

Sam was still trying to sort out the ghost stories and had visions of homeless people stumbling around in the campus tunnels. She wrenched her mind back to the matter at hand.

"What one thing…oh, you mean about Professor Gunn arguing and shouting on the phone? Whatever would that be about, do you think?"

Perhaps it has something to do with money? Do you think he might be a drug pusher? Or possibly he's some kind of thief? Or he could be our murderer?"

"Well, what about our favorite couple?" Sam asked reasonably. "My vote would be that the power people might be behind the murder. Maybe it's pure jealousy? Professor McIntyre was, after all, a rising star in the department. What about our weapons collector? The murder weapon came from his house. He was in the same area as Professor McIntyre."

"Who stood to gain?" Ian said softly. "One has to have something to gain, unless it is a crime of passion. I think we can safely eliminate passion here. I haven't seen much of that, except for our little weapons professor. He and his lady friend seem to have some kind of thing going."

"So, it is, very possibly, about money," Sam was thoughtful. "What kind of money? Are there research rights involved? We can eliminate the crackpot letter. That just doesn't fit in with anything we've seen. Besides, the outside world probably has no clue about what goes on at the University. It has to be someone who is here."

"All good questions," Ian said, wondering just where this investigation was taking them.

Chapter 36

The questions were popping up faster than Sam and Ian could answer them. They decided to go home for dinner and regroup. Perhaps a night off would help to clear their minds.

Ian whipped up a shrimp scampi casserole while Sam made a lettuce salad with spinach, grape tomatoes, sweet onions, olives, and a honey basil dressing and some sour dough bread in their bread machine.

They opened a bottle of Wollersheim River Gold, a Wisconsin wine, and poured two wine glasses half full as they finished preparations for the meal. They intentionally avoided talk of the murder investigation, as they both needed a psychological break. Both felt they should be farther along in the investigation, and in spite of their attempts to be festive, a gloom settled over the kitchen.

Sam snuck a peak at Ian's back muscles rippling under his shirt as he prepared the dish. She was trying to relax, but thoughts of Rob McIntyre and Marie Cavendish intruded into her consciousness, as much as she tried to ignore them. She sighed. That was the reason she had gone into police investigative work. She couldn't stand the injustice in the world and wanted to make a difference. She wondered if she and Ian had made the right decision coming to Madison.

"So, how do you like it here?" She risked a personal question, thinking it might open up lines of communication with Ian.

Ian was on the verge of despair himself, although he would never admit it. He didn't know how to answer. Was Sam unhappy here? Had they made a mistake moving in together? Were they going to fail at this undertaking?

Ian held a spoon in the air as he pondered these questions. After a few minutes, he decided to take the plunge. He couldn't let these questions hang in the air.

"What are you trying to say? Are you unhappy?" He gave Sam a sad smile, as he thought the worst.

"Oh, no," Sam replied in horror, catching the drift of Ian's thoughts. "I didn't mean that at all! I was just wondering if you were comfortable here. I'm very happy with you, and we're pursuing a good thing...I just know it."

"I'm sorry," Ian said. "I'm just tense about this case, and worried that we won't be able to solve it." He let out a sigh of relief. Voicing his worst fears was liberating.

Sam's maternal instincts took over. "I think we're close. We have the suspects boiled down to either the power couple or the visiting professor. We should be smart enough to be able to tip the murderer's hand."

"We need a little help from the outside, and all we're getting at the moment is a deadline set before the police pick up the wrong person. I know that Fred Canon is innocent; of that I'm sure."

"We'll concentrate on that thought," Sam gulped. "Now, let's relax for the time being. We have to eat and sleep...and..."

"I'll take that as a hint for the evening to come," Ian said with a smile. Sam entered the circle of his arms, and the evening proceeded from there. They forgot about their doubts and fears and enjoyed each other's warmth. The outside world slid away in the contentment of the moment.

Chapter 37

The next morning, Sam and Ian received two crucial phone calls as they sat down to eat cereal and orange juice. Sam jumped up to answer the first call. It was from Terry and Nicole.

"Sam, is everything all right? We haven't heard from you for a while. How is the murder investigation going? Are you two safe? We caught some of the news up here, and it sounds like the police are ready to make an arrest. Does that mean you are almost finished?"

Sam's mind registered all of the questions in a split second. Nicole sounded worried, and she didn't want to unduly alarm her.

"Yes, we're fine. The investigation is ready to break, but we need a few more days. We are trying to hold off the arrest the police want to make, because we're certain that they are making a huge mistake. So, no, we're not quite finished. What did you have in mind?"

"We were thinking of coming down to visit you and maybe check out some recording studios in Madison. That way we could do some of our recording there and you wouldn't have to travel so much. We were thinking it might be fun, but we won't come until we get an invite." She broke off uncertainly.

Sam did some fast thinking. She knew that Ian would want to spend time with Terry and Nicole, but they were at such a critical juncture in the case that she didn't want any distractions.

"Can we call you back in a couple of days to fix a time for your visit?" She tried to put as much warmth into her voice as possible, but she didn't fool Nicole.

"You're on to something, aren't you?" Nicole asked. "I'm beginning to recognize the 'we're on the hunt,' note in your voice. We can come down anytime. Just give us a call when your case is settled. Then we'll plan a visit."

Sam breathed an inward sigh of relief. She loved Terry and Nicole, but at the same time she needed all of her energy and resources to finish the case. She should have known that they would be supportive and sensitive enough to figure out what was happening.

"Thanks Nicole. You're the best. You're absolutely right. We're 'hot on the trail' of the bad guy or bad guys. We'll be sure to call you immediately when the case is finished. Thanks for being so understanding! What is new with the wedding plans?"

"We can talk about that when you're able to listen with your entire brain," Nicole laughed. "Until that time, don't worry...everything is under control up here. Talk to ya soon, honey. You and Ian take care of yourselves!"

Sam hung up the phone as Ian came into the room. He gave Sam a hug and nuzzled her neck just a little, which made a shiver run through her body.

"Did I hear you talking to Nicole?" He asked. "Did I get wind of you talking about them making a trip down here? I hope they're not coming tomorrow!"

She smiled mischievously. "We were just planning our 'after the case is solved' visit with them. I told them we'd call them as soon as we have things wrapped up."

Ian nodded. "Good work. I, for one, can only concentrate on one earth-shattering concept at a time. If they came down here in the middle of the case, it could really muck up the works. But I am anxious to see them again."

Before Sam could reply the phone rang again. This time it was for Ian, who picked up the phone and listened for a few minutes, a frown darkening his face. He talked for about five minutes while Sam discreetly busied herself with chores in the kitchen.

Finally Ian stood in the doorway, eyes staring meaningfully at Sam. "That was one of my buddies at the FBI," he began. "It seems that there has been a robbery at the Art Institute…"

"In Minneapolis," Sam finished his sentence. And we just happened to see who there?"

"Nah, couldn't be related," Ian said.

Sam didn't say anything for a few moments while her mind raced to integrate this new piece of information. What would an art theft have to do with the murder of a professor at the University of Wisconsin? At first glance it seemed to be two unrelated events.

She lifted one eyebrow at Ian, in imitation to one of his most potent glances. She waggled her eyebrows meaningfully, and then cracked up.

"Do you think our good professor Helmut Gunn might have a wee bit to do with this chain of events? Or perhaps the 'power couple' is in league with a ring of art thieves? We could begin by talking to someone at the insurance company. They usually have their own investigators before they pay out thousands or millions of dollars? Hmmmm?"

"My very thought," Ian smiled. They were back on the trail, and things were getting interesting indeed.

The next item on their agenda was to place a call to the Art Institute. An administrative assistant who answered their call connected them with the director, a Manfred Helm. After explaining their suspicions to Dr. Helm, he readily agreed to give them the name of their insurance company.

The insurance company, Cosmo, directed them to the Europol website, and they logged on to check out some of the pieces of stolen art listed on their website. Since Ian had worked with a few people in Europol, they decided to e-mail one of his friends within the organization, Pierre Devreau. Ian sent Pierre an e-mail explaining the art theft at the Art Institute and attached a file that Manfred Helm e-mailed to him describing the missing pieces.

All they could do was wait for Pierre's answer. Perhaps he would know something that might help them. Just for good measure, they had included a description of Fred Canon, Tom Jacobs, Phyllis Litchfield, and finally, Helmut Gunn. Pierre would know if any of the four had any involvement with art theft.

They sat down and finished their light breakfast while they waited for an answer to their e-mail to Pierre. Time was so short, and they really needed a break in the case. Sam pulled out her laptop and began to make some notes to help clear her mind. Ian decided to put a dish together for dinner that they could heat up quickly. He had a feeling that the day's events would soon overtake them.

They didn't speak much for an hour, each of them involved in their own thoughts. Neither dared express doubts, because failure was not an idea they would give voice to. Finally Sam broke the silence.

"We're going to have to do some fast surveillance if Pierre gives us a lead. If he doesn't have anything, how are we going to cover our three suspects?"

Ian didn't say anything as he thought over the possibilities. They were going to have to proceed in a logical, well rehearsed manner. There was no room for mistakes.

"We'll start with Helmut. He is European and might have obvious connections. However, we should also check out the power duo one more time. We should also check in with Anni and with Janey McIntyre. We have much to do today, and we can't afford any missteps."

"Why don't I call Anni and ask her what she knows about their schedules?" Sam commented, thinking aloud.

"She can at least tell us when their classes meet and also when their office hours are held. She might also know about their patterns at the office. Some faculty might come in every day; others might only come in once a week. I suppose it depends upon their area of expertise and whether they do their research at home or in their offices."

Ian looked at Sam with admiration. She had an uncanny ability to put herself into other people's shoes, and she also had a natural affinity for various aspects of people's lives. He wouldn't have thought of all that. He gave a quick nod of his head and grinned at Sam.

Sam caught the drift of Ian's thoughts and flushed with pleasure as she dialed Anni's office number.

"Anni, Sam here. Can you give us the schedules of Drs. Gunn, Litchfield, and Jacobs? No, we don't have anything concrete yet, but we're running down some leads. Don't say anything to anyone there if they ask. We'll be in touch soon."

Chapter 38

Sam dialed Janey McIntyre's number. Janey answered on the second ring, and the relief at hearing from Sam and Ian was evident in her voice.

"I understand that the police are ready to make an arrest. They just made an announcement on the local news. Do you know who the murderer is?" Her voice cracked with the strain. "I just want to put all of this behind me."

Janey's obvious anguish pulled at Sam's conscience. She didn't want to let Janey down, but she couldn't stand the thought of the police making a big mistake.

"Janey," she began. "We're not sure that the police actually have the right person. We're waiting to hear about something that might be related to the case. If our hunch is correct, it just might break the case. But we wanted to touch base with you and make sure you are all right. We think that we're very close to finding the murderer."

Janey gasped. "What do you mean? You think that the police are arresting the wrong man? I couldn't imagine a more odious thing happening! I would have to go through a trial, and an innocent man might be ruined."

Sam felt totally helpless. She had meant to reassure Janey, and she was making a mess of the attempt. She cast her mind about for some phrases that would console Janey.

"Janey, listen to me," Sam put as much urgency into her voice as she could muster. "We are going to break this case, and very soon. Ian is waiting for an e-mail from one of his friends in Europol that might just lead us in the right direction. Please don't lose heart. We have already talked with Joel Drake, and he is as interested in arresting the murderer as we are. He is under a lot of pressure to solve the crime, but he is completely trustworthy. I'm sure this will be resolved correctly. Just hang in there!"

Sam waited for a few more minutes while Janey composed herself.

"Sam, you're right. I trust you and Ian, and I'll just sit tight, unless you want me to do something. It's just hard waiting...I'm not used to not being in control."

"Attagirl. You're one of the most courageous women I've ever met. Think positive. I know that this will turn out all right. We'll call you again as soon as we know something. If you think of anything that might help, or if someone from the department calls you and seems to be acting strangely, call us immediately. Do you think you can handle that?"

Janey gave a final sniff, signaling her returning composure. "Damn straight. We'll get the son of a bitch."

Sam heaved a sigh of relief. Janey was back in fighting form. Now it was up to her and Ian to finish the job.

* * * * *

It took less than an hour after Sam's conversation with Janey for Ian's computer to beep that it had incoming mail. Ian dashed over to the computer and opened his "in" basket online. There was an e-mail from Pierre Devreau.

"Ian, old buddy, I haven't heard from you for months, but the grapevine says that you have found a lady love. I'll have to meet her...she must be really something to have settled you down, you dog! Now as to the matter of your request about the art theft, I think I have an answer for you. We have had a report of an art theft at the Minneapolis Art Institute that coincides with your visit. Three pieces were stolen; one is a Picasso, and we are waiting for it to turn up on the official arts market. The thief will probably wait for at least six months, maybe more. It is a very valuable and famous piece of art.

That is all we know at the moment. We'll be in touch with any further developments. Please share any information you may turn up on your end. Regards to you, and good luck on the hunt." He signed it "Your ol' buddy Pierre."

Ian sat back after he had finished reading the e-mail. That clinched it. Their thief must be Helmut Gunn. But was he also the murderer? What connection would Helmut Gunn have with Rob McIntyre? It was still a puzzle.

Ian sent a quick e-mail back to Pierre telling him that he might have a line on the art thief and that he would get back to him when he had more information.

Sam had crept up behind Ian and read the message from Pierre. It didn't surprise her a bit. She had pegged Helmut Gunn as a bad sort the moment she laid eyes on him.

"But is he our murderer?" She gave voice to the questions that were floating around in Ian's mind. He turned around and put his arm around her.

"This could be very dangerous, you know," he said. "If Gunn gets wind of the fact that we are on to him, there is no telling what he will do. From now on we'll need to be armed every time we leave the house."

Sam shivered in spite of herself. Armed meant that all sorts of possibilities could be in the wind, and also that they had placed both Anni and possibly Janey in even more peril.

"We need to finish this," she said, her eyes glittering.

Chapter 39

After an hour of discussion, Sam and Ian decided they had to search Helmut Gunn's office. They could safely break into his apartment, but if they could find something that would be incriminating in his office on campus, they could take that information to the police.

"Why don't we go out tonight, and maybe we could cruise by Helmut Gunn's place again," Sam said innocently, but there was no mistaking her meaning."

"Good idea," Ian said uneasily, feeling impatient. He knew they were under considerable pressure to break the case, but he didn't want to worry Sam by freaking out himself. Looking at her sideways he knew he wasn't fooling her.

A casual drive by Helmut Gunn's apartment showed nothing out of the ordinary. Frustrated, they headed for home. Neither said a word until they got out of the van and went into the house. Cleo and Quincy wrapped themselves around their legs and meowed to show their concern.

Sam put her hand on his arm. She didn't say anything, but gave his arm a gentle squeeze. Ian reacted by sliding his arm around her. They took refuge in each other for the evening and fell into a deep sleep with kitties curled up on the bed.

The following morning dawned sunny and pleasant, with temperatures projected to rise to the upper seventies. There was a gentle breeze, and the late summer sun was warming without being intrusive. It was a perfect fall day on a campus swarming with excited students.

After a quick breakfast of cereal and orange juice, they make another trek into the Philosophy Department.

Sam and Ian were both dressed in campus casual, jeans and loose fitting tops. Sam's pale blue pullover set off her red hair perfectly, and she looked like a model on the lam. She attracted more than a few appreciative glances from students on campus. Ian was no less resplendent in his attire, and although he noticed the glances at Sam, he was attracting just as much attention. Students wondered if there was another movie being shot on campus. Madison has been the site of several big movies in the past twenty years.

Sam had already attended her law class for the day. She had to go to the library that afternoon to catch up on some reading. She felt like she was being torn in ten different directions, and she knew Ian felt the same way. They hadn't counted on their lives becoming so complicated, but neither of them would back down from their commitments, of that she was sure.

Anni was knee-deep in papers when they walked into her office. She had her usual cup of coffee sitting on her desk. The outer office of the Philosophy department was full of commotion. Students wandered in to add late classes. Faculty came in to check their mail and chat with the staff. The department had a congenial atmosphere, where the faculty interacted with staff on a friendly basis and didn't try to distance themselves because of their rank.

"Anni, how's it going?" Sam gave her cousin a jovial smile as she and Ian glided into her office. Anni looked up gratefully. She had been feeling very nervous, and she had the distinct feeling that the investigation was once again centering on her department. She felt loyalty to Sam as her relative, and family came first. But she didn't want to see any sort of negative publicity come to her beloved department. It was a case of classic cognitive dissonance, she reflected to herself wryly remembering her own psychology courses from college.

"Maybe I should be asking you that question?" Anni retorted with a smile. "The very fact that you are here standing in my office is, shall we say, telling? Dare I ask what's new? Do I want to know?"

Sam gave her cousin a reassuring look. She understood what a terrible position Anni was in and could only guess at what she was thinking. But she also knew that Anni was firmly entrenched in her department and that, whatever happened, she was sure that Anni wouldn't suffer any adverse consequences. At least she hoped so.

"We're here to ask another favor," Ian gave Anni the same sympathetic look. "We'd like to search Helmut Gunn's office, if he isn't around."

Anni had been dreading this, but at the same time she was just as determined as Sam and Ian. She remembered her childhood when she and Sam would get together and work on detective cases. At the time, they'd been lighthearted. Anni liked to dress up as Annie Oakley, never realizing that Annie wasn't a detective. Her parents never destroyed her illusion. This was real.

"I'd better clear it with Bruce," she said.

* * * * *

"Just tell them to be careful, and make certain that Helmut isn't around," Bruce told Anni when she called him with Sam and Ian's plan.

"This could be very dangerous," Anni said, when she returned to them. She could feel that Sam and Ian were getting close to the end of their case, and she was certain that Helmut Gunn had something to do with it. Of course, there was still the question of the power couple. Suddenly her head felt like it would explode and she reached for Advil.

Helmut's office looked similar to the day they had visited him. He was on the neat side of the professorial messy versus organized propensities. The top of his desk was virtually bare, with the regulation yellow state message pad, a phone, an answering machine, and his computer.

A search of his desk revealed nothing out of the ordinary, but when they turned his computer on another story emerged. Anni kept a list of all of the passwords for the faculty in the department, and she nervously typed Helmut's user name and password into the computer while Sam and Ian waited impatiently. They didn't want Helmut to walk in and find them going through his computer files.

"I'd rather not be in the room while you conduct your search, so I'll just return to my office. That way I can be a lookout for you," she said nervously, as she slipped out of the chair and dashed out the door.

Sam took Anni's place at the computer and brought up a directory of files. Helmut's directory included syllabi for various courses, papers, e-mail, notes, and pictures.

"I wonder what pictures he has," Sam said, placing the cursor on one of the files and hitting return. The picture that came up was a reproduction of a Picasso. Sam drew in her breath involuntarily and let out a gasp.

Ian looked over Sam's shoulder and emitted a small curse. He bet that that was the Picasso that was missing from the Art Institute.

It might just be a coincidence," Ian said. "Keep looking. We need more proof than this."

The next file Sam opened left no doubt. It was a letter offering the Picasso for sale, with a dollar figure attached.

"Well, I'll be damned. The guy is an art thief," Ian said. "I should have known something was up with him."

Sam quickly printed a copy of the picture and the letter. As it slowly churned out of the copy machine, Anni appeared at the door, a panicked look on her face.

"He just came into the office! I think you'd better get out of her fast," she hissed. Sam had already snatched the incriminating piece of evidence and was shutting down the computer.

She and Ian stepped into the hallway and managed to turn the corner when they heard Helmut's footsteps on the linoleum floor. They beat him by just seconds.

Dashing down the back stairway, Sam and Ian felt sure that Helmut hadn't detected their presence. Wordlessly they got into their van and sped to their house. It seemed a much safer place to be than the department. They needed to talk about this new development and figure out just what it meant to the murder case.

Sam dialed Joel Drake's phone number. He needed to know about their discovery, and they wanted to warn him about not making any premature arrest. Joel answered on the first ring in a weary voice. The case was taking its toll on him, and his voice was scratchy and terse.

"Talk to me," he simply said in a tired voice tinged with hope. He wanted someone…anyone to give him something that would give this case structure.

"Joel," Sam said. "I think we've got something! Did you talk to Europol?"

"I talked to them yesterday," Joel admitted. "Their big thing right now is tracking down stolen art form the Iraq art museums. There are thousands of pieces missing, and they show up on the market every few months. I don't think they even heard what I asked them. But they did say they would call if they discovered anything." He emitted a heavy sigh that hung on the line like an orphaned dog. He hadn't even noticed the excitement in Sam's voice.

"What do you have? Tell me you have something significant so we can solve this case!"

"We have to see you right away," Sam said breathlessly. "We've got something that'll knock your socks off. We think that Professor Helmut Gunn is an art thief. The question is, is he also our murderer?"

"Be here in half an hour," Joel said shortly and hung up. Sam didn't have to second guess him this time.

She and Ian tore out of the house, kitties skittering out of the way, and dashed into their van. They sped over to the police station and were ushered in to Joel's office. Joel looked up expectantly and gave them a broad smile.

"I just called Europol again," he said. "They are waiting for us to fax them whatever information you've brought in. Let's see what you have."

Sam produced the photocopy of the Picasso entitled "Bust De Femme Au Chapeau (Bust of a Woman in a Hat) and waited for Joel's reaction. Joel looked at the photocopy and went online to the Europol website. Sure enough, the Minneapolis Art Institute had already transmitted a picture of the missing painting. They matched.

"Well, I'll be damned," he said and broke into a grin. "I think we have an art thief on our hands, and it shouldn't be too hard to shake him out of his tree. The question is, is he also our murderer? We'll have to proceed cautiously."

Joel picked up the phone and barked into the receiver like it was a recalcitrant child. "Howe, you and Smith get into my office pronto." He slammed down the phone and turned grim. "We've got to act fast, before this guy figures out what we're doing."

The two officers appeared at his door. "Howe, I want you to get a search warrant for Professor Helmut Gunn's apartment. Smith, I want you and Gardner to pick up Professor Gunn and bring him in for questioning. I would really like to hear what the good professor has to say about his actions." His mouth turned up into a smirk.

He turned back to Sam and Ian. "Ian, I understand you have some connections to Europol. Could you give your friend a call and find out if there have been art thefts when Helmut Gunn has been in Germany? I understand he's from the University of Bonn."

Ian nodded, impressed that Joel Drake was current with information about their possible suspects. He must have been listening to Sam and him closer than they'd thought. Ian gave Joel a tight smile and nodded.

"Now, mind you, I still don't know that there is any connection between Professor Gunn and the murders," Joel admonished, eyes on Sam. "But we'll keep our eyes open. I still think we have our murder suspect. We have to assume that there could be two different culprits until we find something that disproves my theory."

Sam's eyes hardened at Joel's final statements. Her skepticism must have shown on her face, because Joel pointed a finger at her and shook his head. She groaned. An innocent man was relying on their ability to solve the case.

"Let's go," she said grimly to Ian. His mouth was set in a thin line.

"I really don't like that Helmut Gunn," he said, feeling his right hand curl into a fist.

"Yeah, me neither," Sam replied. "But we need more proof."

Chapter 40

Everyone dashed off to obey Joel Drake's orders. Dan Howe reported back to Joel, saying that the judge was in the middle of a trial, but that he would take a recess if they would pick up the search warrant from his secretary and take it over for him to sign. Dan was about 5'11" and had curly brown hair, a well-defined chin, and chocolate brown eyes. Dan was a big country music fan and frequented the bars during his off hours where he was very popular with the ladies with his line-dancing ability.

Howe's partner, Michael Smith, stood at 6'2", and weighed 210 pounds. He had jet black hair and brilliant blue eyes that could be angelically gentle or turn steely when danger threatened. Most people didn't push him around.

Two hours passed, during which Sam and Ian used Sam's laptop to get hold of Pierre Devreau by e-mail. The department had just installed a wireless router, so Sam didn't have to borrow any of the departmental computers. She had scanned the copy of the Picasso into her computer and attached it to the e-mail to Devreau.

Joel decided that they shouldn't pick up Helmut Gunn until they'd had a chance to search his apartment. They didn't want to tip him off that they were suspicious of him and wanted to keep their actions low key.

Sam called Anni to see when Helmut taught, and was gratified to learn that he had a three hour seminar. She thought that he held office hours for at least an hour after that, so he would be busy for a while.

Sam reported back to Joel, who passed the information on to Dan Smith. The schedule was going to be tight, but if everything worked out, they could manage it. The judge, whose name was William Stowe, called Dan Howe, saying he was ready for him. The secretary who worked for him, Suzy Larson, had just finished running the search warrant off. Dan dashed out the door with Michael Smith. They would radio for backup to meet over at Helmut Smith's apartment.

Sam was pacing around the office, checking her e-mail every ten minutes for an answer from Pierre. Finally, there was the "you've got mail" announcement from her laptop, and she raced over to open the missive. She scanned the e-mail and turned to Ian excitedly.

"It took Pierre a while, because he had to call the Department of Philosophy to check Helmut Gunn's appointments. Fortunately their computer system is easy to access, and the departmental secretary faxed him Joel's complete record. Guess what? There have been three separate art thefts during the times that Helmut has been in residence. Pierre is very excited. He thinks we've stumbled upon a ring of art thieves. We're to keep him updated!"

"Yes," Ian said, his spirits restored. They were finally making some headway.

Joel was just as excited. "If nothing else, this could crack open a major International art theft ring. I've just sent Dan and Michael over to pick up the search warrant. We should know in a couple of hours. There is nothing else you can do for the moment. Why don't you go home and I'll call you when we're finished with the search of Gunn's apartment?"

That last comment shocked Sam a little, as she was used to being involved in snagging suspects. But she could understand. She and Ian were now private detectives, and they couldn't be involved in the police procedure. Still, it stung. She smiled ruefully. It couldn't be helped. Sam put her hand on Ian's arm. "Come on, Ian, let's get out of here. We still have work to do." They walked out of Joel's office, suddenly feeling irrelevant.

"Would you like to take a walk, and then go get some coffee?" Ian asked, suddenly feeling Sam's prickliness. He thought he understood what she was feeling. They had just handed much of the case over to the police, and they were a little unsure as to what to do next.

Sam grunted assent, and they decided to take a walk along the lake path and retrace their steps. It was a glorious fall day, the sun was streaming warming rays on to happy students, and the Memorial Union terrace, which featured colorful tables and chairs overlooking Lake Mendota, was full to capacity. It was Friday, and the next day the University of Wisconsin Badger football team was slated to play. There was a palpable excitement in the air, and the mood was decidedly festive. Sam only felt glum.

Ian let her work through her mood. He understood that she felt detached from the action and admitted to himself that his own thoughts and feelings were running along the same lines. He consoled himself with the idea that the end of the case was near and that he and Sam would be able to return to the original plan. Sam could continue with her law classes and he could return to the band.

Finally Sam broke the silence. She might have been talking to herself, and Ian almost missed her comments.

"So, what proof do we have that Helmut Gunn is anything but an art thief? That doesn't necessarily make him a murderer. He may not have anything to do with the murders, but it would be too much of a coincidence," she fretted, wringing her hands in a gesture that Ian hadn't seen her use before.

"Don't forget that Helmut's office was right next door to Rob McIntyre's," Ian reminded her, without thinking. He was beginning to worry about Sam.

Sam bristled. "I know that! I'm just trying to work out a theory here. Perhaps Rob overheard Helmut talking on the phone, or maybe he passed by his office at the wrong time," she postulated.

"People don't usually murder someone who just happens to be in the hallway, unless that person witnesses something," Ian reminded her.

"Maybe Rob walked by accidentally when Helmut had the stolen picture in his office?" Sam hypothesized. "No, I doubt that Helmut would have brought the stolen painting to his office. It would be too risky."

"Do you think that Rob could have been blackmailing Helmut? That would presuppose a certain relationship between the two. Helmut was only here for one semester. I can't imagine that he would have gotten close to Helmut in that amount of time. Of course, Phyllis Litchfield and Tom Jacobs have supposedly had a friendship with Helmut. Maybe it has something to do with them."

"Do you want to talk to them again," Ian asked, suddenly alert. Sam's line of thought was suddenly making too much sense. Maybe there was another piece to this puzzle they were missing entirely.

"Absolutely," Sam said, a slow smile spreading across her features. They had another mission.

* * * * *

They found Phyllis Litchfield and Tom Jacobs in their adjoining offices, talking excitedly. They looked up in disgust as Sam and Ian rounded the corner and approached.

"Oh, God, here come the sleuths," Phyllis said sarcastically to Tom with enough volume so that Sam and Ian couldn't help but overhear. "What a bore, I mean, really. What could they want with us?"

"I'll take care of those two right now," Tom said, charging out of his office with a menacing scowl.

He invaded Ian's space, planting his feet about six inches from Ian's and pushing him on the shoulder.

"See, here, we don't have anything further to talk to you about. Why don't you get lost, asshole?"

Ian gave him a little push in the chest, which caused him to back up back into his office.

"Hey! What's the meaning of this," Tom scowled. "If you don't leave immediately, I'm calling security." It was an empty threat, and his eyes showed it.

"We have just a few more questions for you," Sam said in a low voice, trying to calm him down. "At this very minute the police are searching your friend, Helmut Gunn's, apartment. They think that perhaps Helmut is mixed up in an art theft ring, and perhaps he is also the murderer. We're just wondering what your relationship is with Helmut and if you might possibly be involved in this mess." She gave Tom her brightest smile, but her eyes remained menacing.

Tom glanced quickly over at Phyllis. She glared back at him and they remained oblivious to Sam and Ian while they mentally communicated. Phyllis' gaze became insistent, and after a few minutes Tom capitulated to the obvious power she wielded over him.

"Yes," he admitted. "Helmut is our friend. He has supplied me with pot for years, but that is all. We are not involved in any art theft ring, and we certainly are not involved in any murder. What is the harm in smoking a little weed? I'm a very anxious person, and it helps me to relax. Phyllis and I argue about it constantly, but it is my little vice. Helmut seems able to get it for me with very few questions asked. But I swear to you that I am not a murderer or a thief. What Helmut does with his time is anyone's guess. He has not associated with the rest of the faculty."

Tom had started to shake with his admission. He raised tortured eyes to Phyllis, who went over and patted him on the back and began to talk to him in soothing tones.

"Tom, for your own good, you need to stay away from Helmut Gunn. I've told you that I don't like him. He makes me nervous. And now this! He is undoubtedly an art thief, and perhaps he murdered our colleague!"

Phyllis looked over at Sam and Ian. "We have been trying to cover this up ever since you arrived. It has been ruining our lives. Please don't tell anyone that you've had this conversation with us. It could destroy our reputations, and we might lose our positions here at the University."

Sam glanced at Ian, who was frowning, his mind working furiously. A few minutes passed, and he made no comment. But Sam knew what he was thinking. Tom Jacob's mistakes, while foolhardy, were not high on the scale of law enforcement. However, when one bought drugs, they often interacted with bigger fish that the FBI and other law enforcement agencies would be interested in. Inwardly Sam figured they had stumbled on to something big.

Ian turned towards Tom, with a reproving look in his eye. "All right, this is what we're going to do. You are going to keep tabs on Helmut Gunn for us. We want to know any moves he makes. Since we have not witnessed you committing any crime and only have your say so for what's transpired, we'll cut you some slack. But, be warned, if you try to double-cross us in any way, the deal's off!"

Tom stood unmoving for a few minutes as he digested the deal that Ian had offered. He had lived with fear and paranoia for years, and felt that his world was shattering before his very eyes. He gave a deep shuddering sigh and finally nodded his head, unable to speak for a moment. When he got hold of himself, he had one question.

"What exactly do you want us to do?"

Sam had an idea. "We want you to invite Helmut over to your house for dinner. We'll speak to the Madison Police about fixing you up with a wire. We would like you to be subtle, but to pump Professor Gunn for information about his plans and activities. Do you think you can do that?"

Phyllis looked up. "We'll do anything you ask. I'm hoping that my husband has learned his lesson from this series of events. But we'd like to cooperate. If Helmut Gunn is a thief and a murderer, the sooner we can entrap him, the better! Yes, I think we can pull this off!"

"Let me clear this with Joel Drake first, and we'd better hurry!" Sam whipped out her cell phone and dialed Joel's number.

Joel answered on the first ring. After Sam explained their plan, he hedged.

"We may be putting the good professors at risk," he complained. This would mean that we would have to delay searching Helmut's home until tomorrow. But, if you think this would be helpful, I'll give you that time. Just tell them to be careful. We don't want to case unraveling before our very eyes!"

Sam flipped her phone shut and looked at Tom and Phyllis. "Okay, this is what we're going to do," she said.

Phyllis and Tom listened to the plan with their minds swirling. Double-crossing Helmut Gunn might endanger their lives, and they wanted to know what they were getting into before they agreed with the plan. But at the same time, they had to grudgingly admire Sam and Ian as they laid out the plan for the evening. When she finished, they agreed to go along with the venture.

"But if you put my wife in jeopardy, I'll see to it that your licenses are suspended," Tom threatened as his courage came back.

"Just do your part," Sam assured him. "I can't guarantee perfect results, but you two may end up looking like heroes. That would certainly be an improvement over facing a possible scandal over drug use."

Chapter 41

Inviting Helmut Gunn over for dinner proved to be a relatively easy task. Phyllis was a gourmet chef, and Helmut had eaten at their table on more than one occasion.

Sam and Ian met Phyllis and Tom at the police station, where Tom would be fitted with a wire. Tom was very nervous, but Phyllis' eyes sparkled with anticipation.

"This is all quite irregular," she cooed. "But I think we can pull it off. We're both big mystery buffs, you know." Tom looked at her with misgiving, but went along without comment.

"Just don't take any chances," Joel Drake advised. "Keep up the conversation, and try to ask leading questions. Get Helmut to talk about himself. Maybe he'll slip something in that will be useful. Ask him about his interests…what he does in his spare time."

Joel couldn't quite figure out how Sam and Ian had roped Phyllis and Tom into this little masquerade, but he wasn't asking questions. It might prove to be very useful, although they probably wouldn't be able to use recorded conversations in court. Still, he had agreed to go along with the plan, because there was still a murderer to catch. He trusted Sam and Ian's instincts.

Joel had suggested that Sam and Ian remain outside in the stakeout van, which was fully equipped for surveillance. Sam put together a "roughing it" bag, with sandwiches, pop, water, chips, flashlights, and their guns. The van had a porta-potty, so they wouldn't have to worry about facilities.

The day flew by with dinner preparations, with Phyllis assembling sesame ginger chicken with hot cooked

Japanese curly noodles, Italian chopped salad, and a mocha torte for dessert. They would drink a Chardonnay for Phyllis and various kinds of beer for the men.

Both Phyllis and Tom were desperately nervous, but they tried hard not to show it. Tom straightened the house and helped with the salad. He ran to the liquor store to pick up liquid refreshments. He bought himself a bottle of Southern Comfort…an apt name, he thought to himself as he paid for his purchases.

"Open ended questions," Phyllis muttered to herself as she mixed ingredients. "No slip-ups…"

"Precisely," Tom countered in a stentorial tone, but inwardly he quaked.

* * * * *

Meanwhile, Sam and Ian were preparing for their stakeout. They would accompany Dan Howe and Michael Smith. The Madison Police Department had a fully equipped van with all the comforts, Sam thought to herself. It would be a little cramped, but her excitement at once again being part of the action far outweighed any bodily inconvenience.

They arrived approximately one hour before Helmut Gunn's anticipated arrival time. A test of the audio equipment was successful, and they settled back to wait, opening bottles of water to stay hydrated.

Helmut appeared in his used silver Toyota Camry about one half hour later. He emerged from his car carrying a bottle of wine. He stood about 6'2", had thick blond hair cut very short and square jaw. He looked like the epitome of Hitler youth, or a bad guy out of a James Bond movie Sam thought to herself, gazing at him. She was sure that he would be a formidable enemy.

"It's show time," Ian said through clenched teeth. "I sure hope this guy incriminates himself with something we can use against him. I'd sure like to nail his ass. I'd lay odds that he is our killer."

Sam responded only with a nod. Dan and Mike both chuckled in reaction to Ian's comments. Dan was fiddling with the knobs of the transmission equipment, and finally pulled in a strong signal.

"Hello out there...can you hear me?" Tom Jacobs whispered into his wire.

"You're coming in just fine," Sam assured him. "Don't be nervous, and try to draw him out as much as possible." Her comments were cut off as the sound of footsteps heralded the beginning of the evening.

"You have a beautiful house; not too cluttered. You obviously have excellent taste. I always enjoy being here," Helmut commented as he entered the room. The usual pleasantries were exchanged, and they sat down for a drink. The conversation began slowly, but soon a party atmosphere prevailed as the alcohol began to flow.

Phyllis threw out the first of a series of open-ended questions. "What research are you doing during this trip, Helmut? You lead such a fascinating life."

"Just more of the same," Helmut said dryly. "Academia does take up the lion's share of one's time, don't you think?"

"Do you have other hobbies?" Tom interjected.

"Oh, yes, the usual, I love opera, art, jogging..." Helmut replied shortly.

"Who is your favorite opera star, and what kind of art do you like?" Phyllis persisted. She gave Helmut a half smile of interest, trying to keep her questions casual.

"Oh, I don't know," Helmut said. "Any type of opera...I especially like "The Phantom of the Opera," and "Les Mis," but I also enjoy the older operas. As for art, I love French Impressionist, Modern, such as Picasso, Pre-Raphaelites, such as Waterhouse, almost anything." He gave Phyllis a look which said "your serve."

"Well, give me rock n' roll anytime," Tom decided to end that particular line of questioning for the moment. He didn't want to tip Helmut off that there were people listening in to the conversation.

"Do you think that Fred Canon could possibly have murdered Rob McIntyre?" Phyllis asked Helmut, after a brief period of silence. "He just doesn't seem the type to me. Did you know Rob McIntyre?"

"Well, no, on both counts," Helmut said quietly but with sudden deadly calm. "Why do you ask?"

Phyllis gave a short, nervous laugh. "I suppose I am being macabre. Please pardon me. It's simply that it's on everyone's mind. I hope it all ends soon." She gave an outward shudder. "We want to return to our normal routine." She tried to give Helmut an endearing smile.

The meal continued with few comments. After a suitable after dinner liquor, Helmut took his leave. Tom shut the door after him with a sigh of relief. He didn't think that they'd given away their position, but one never knows.

"Oh, by the way," Helmut said over his shoulder as he walked out the door, "you should be careful what questions you ask a person. It just might get you into trouble." He gave them a steely look as he walked out the door. The air seemed to suck out of the room.

"That went fairly well," Tom commented to Phyllis, who promptly burst into tears.

"Do you think he knew we were taping him? I was just sure that he would pull out a gun on us," Phyllis cried.

Tom put his arm around her shoulder and gave her an awkward pat while his mind raced.

A short time later the doorbell rang. Sam and Ian stood on the threshold giving Tom and Phyllis a reassuring smile. Phyllis stood frozen as she opened the door.

"May we come in? We thought you might like to debrief after your experience. We want to thank you for participating. You did just fine," Sam said reassuringly.

"Of course," Tom said, motioning them in and steering them into the living room, where they sat down on two matching overstuffed chairs.

"Do you think that Helmut was threatening us?" Phyllis demanded when they sat down. She sat glumly in a chair gulping down a drink. She couldn't control her shaking and wondered if they'd just made themselves a target. She was sorry they'd participated and was angry.

"We'll need to tread very carefully," Sam said. "It's hard to know what he knows, but I think it's time for the police to pick him up for questioning." Phyllis and Tom nodded glumly and grabbed for each other. Phyllis buried her head into Tom's shoulder and wept.

Sam pulled out her cell phone to call Joel Drake. She felt that the time was right for the police to make their move. Joel's phone was busy, so she punched the cell phone and sat down to try to reassure Phyllis and Tom.

"You've done a good thing tonight," she began. "Helmut didn't exactly give away his position, but his hints were very revealing. The question is, is he on to us?"

She nervously pulled out her cell phone again. She needed to know what was happening with the police before they could make any additional decisions. The phone was once again busy. She punched her phone off with a sigh and a twinge of apprehension.

A moment later her cell phone rang, and she answered immediately. Her heart began to pound as she said a quick "Hello?"

"Sam, I've been trying to get hold of you," Joel said, sounding breathless. "How did the wiretap go?"

"This guy's a cool customer, but he did make a veiled threat to Tom and Phyllis," Sam said. "I think it would be a good idea to bring him in for questioning."

"We're going to do more than that," Joel growled. "Do you want to be in on the interview? It might be mutually beneficial for both of us. We'll give him enough time to get home and pick him up."

"Absolutely," Sam said. "We need to get this guy off of the street. But from what I heard during that dinner, he's a cool customer. We might need more evidence than we've got." She chewed on a hangnail that suddenly throbbed.

"I'm sure the search warrant will take care of that," Joel replied. "Don't worry, we're on top of this case."

Chapter 42

There wasn't much to do except to go home to wait for Joel Drake's call. They didn't hear anything and finally went to bed. They both immediately fell into a deep sleep.

The next morning Sam decided to check in with both Janey and Anni. She dialed Janey's number to give her an update. Janey was off for the day and answered immediately. Sam filled her in on the events of the last few days.

"So, you think this guy murdered my husband?" Janey said in a hushed voice.

"We think so, but we need more evidence. The police have a search warrant for his home and computer, and they can also use it to check his office," Sam replied. "Ian and I will be there while the police question him. If there is anything you can think of that might be relevant, call us right away. It just might help to put the lid on this thing."

"Let me think about that for a while and I'll call you back," Janey said. Sam replaced the receiver and sat down to talk to Ian.

"She just might come up with something," she told Ian. "I have a good feeling about this, but we'll need more than that. I wish there was something concrete that we had in our possession. Damn!" She suddenly felt angry and impatient.

"You'd better check on Anni," Ian reminded her softly, sensing her mood. "We want to make sure she is also safe while we conclude our business with Helmut Gunn."

"You're right," Sam said, as she picked up the phone to dial Anni's work number. Anni didn't answer the phone, and instead Sam got the receptionist.

"We haven't seen Anni today," she told Sam. "She didn't call in, which is quite unusual. We tried her house, but there was no answer there either. We're afraid that something might have happened to her. Can you check on her for us? It would certainly ease the anxiety around here. We're hearing all sorts of weird gossip, and we don't know what is going on."

"Oh, shit," Sam said, as her stomach suddenly lurched. She quickly concluded the phone call promising to report back with any information. It didn't make sense. Where was Anni?

"What's going on?" Ian demanded as Sam punched the off button.

"Anni didn't report in for work today," Sam answered tersely as she dialed Anni's number at her apartment. There was no answer.

"I think that Helmut may have kidnapped Anni. Maybe he got suspicious after the dinner party last night. But why take Anni?" Sam started to pace.

"Well, I don't think he took a liking to us," Ian said quietly. "We must have hit a nerve. So he's taken the offensive. He's obviously got something big to hide."

"Anni never misses work," Sam said. "I don't want to wait to find out what's happened to her. We've got to do something." She stared out the window.

"Take it easy, Sam. We'll find her," Ian said, joining Sam, who had gone completely still. Then the tears came.

Chapter 43

The phone rang again, and Sam rushed to answer it. It was Joel Drake.

"I've got four officers over at Helmut Gunn's apartment," he said. "Don't worry, I'm sure they'll find something that ties him to the murder. I'll call you back as soon as we've got him in custody."

"It may not be that simple," Sam said soberly. "I think that Helmut Gunn has kidnapped Anni. She didn't show up at work today, and no one has been able to reach her. We're on our way over to her apartment right now."

"I'll send two officers to meet you there...and one of them is going to be me," Joel snarled. "If that asshole has kidnapped Anni, he's going to feel the wrath of quite a few people." He was breathing hard as he finished his speech.

"Meet you there in a half hour," Sam said.

"Make it twenty minutes," Joel answered. "I take it you have a key to get in? We want to make sure that she hasn't hurt herself and is lying unconscious on the floor."

Twenty-five minutes later Sam and Ian met Joel at Anni's apartment. Sam stifled a gasp as they entered the door. Anni's immaculate apartment had been turned topsy-turvy, with drawers carelessly tossed on the floor, papers tossed from her computer desk onto the floor, and chairs overturned.

Sam and Ian took in the grim scene with fury. There had obviously been a struggle, and the place was a mess. Sam comforted herself with the thought that at least there weren't huge amounts of blood smeared around. She felt sure that her cousin was still alive. She just had to be. Sam didn't know what she would do if something happened to Anni. She was like a sister.

Joel was on the phone calling for a crime scene investigation team. They didn't have long to wait. The photographer was the first to arrive, and Joel's team had already placed yellow tape outside of Anni's door. The photographer, whose name was Earl Withers, began taking pictures of Anni's apartment. Stan Case and Joe Deneen dusted for fingerprints while Joel and Sam tried to reconstruct the scene.

"I wonder if he was looking for something," Sam said, surveying the damage.

"I don't think so," Joel answered. "I think this guy is simply a bully and wanted to prove how strong and smart he is. I want to tear him apart myself."

"We'll do it together," Sam said venomously. She was looking around for anything that might give them a clue as to Anni's whereabouts. There was nothing. Her stomach did a few flip flops, and she went into the bathroom and was sick. Ian was right behind her, trying not to touch her but making sure she was all right.

"I want my cousin back," Sam said finally, after she rinsed her mouth. She used some of Anni's toothpaste to get rid of the foul stench she tasted. "I want to hurt this guy. I want to hurt him bad."

Ian took his cue and put his arms around Sam. "That makes two of us," he said, giving her back little pats of reassurance. "Don't worry. We've got the entire Madison police force on our side. We've got the FBI, and Europol. This creep is not going to slip through our fingers. We'll get him Sam, and we'll get Anni back. Now, it's time for us to pull ourselves together and get to work."

Sam gave Ian a grateful look. He had just pulled her out of a black depression with a few sentences. She was falling deeper and deeper in love with him and wanted him to know how grateful she was and how impressed she was with him.

"Ian Temple, have I told you that I love you completely and forever?" She made the statement in low and forceful tones.

Ian was so shocked he didn't know what to say for a moment. Had she actually said what he thought he heard? He didn't dare ask her to repeat it and pondered for a moment trying to find words that could convey his feeling without scaring her off.

"I've loved you from the moment I laid eyes on you, Sam Peters," he finally said. "I've never told a woman that I loved her before, and when I fall in love, it's for keeps. Now, let's go get your cousin back from that monster. I think I have some ideas where to look."

"This time we're going armed," Sam replied in low tones. "I'm not taking any chances."

Chapter 44

Anni woke up with a start. Her arms were bound behind her back and she was laying on some kind of stone floor. She couldn't move her feet and assumed they were also tied. Her shoulders ached and she was getting a headache. She hoped it wouldn't turn into a migraine but she had a history of them and could feel the signs.

She couldn't remember what had happened to get her into this position and felt a wave of panic and nausea. Had she been kidnapped? She could barely remember who she was, and she was cold. She had a pair of jeans and a sweatshirt on, but the dampness penetrated her clothes, causing her to shiver.

She tried to move and felt only pain. She groaned and tried to settle into a comfortable position, but couldn't find one. She was afraid she would throw up and tried to take deep breaths to overcome the sensation.

"Ah, you're awake," a voice came from behind her. She couldn't move anything but her head and wasn't sure she wanted to turn around to see who was. She tried to remember what could have happened to land her in this predicament.

"Who are you, and where am I? Why am I tied up?" She tried to sound demanding, but her throat was parched. "I'm afraid I'm going to throw up. Can I have some water?"

"Only if you're nice and don't try to fight," the voice of Helmut Gunn with its German accent boomed in her ears. She winced at the volume of his voice and gave another moan. She didn't dare ask him what he intended to do with her. She couldn't think about that yet.

Helmut walked around so he was standing in front of her. He had a plastic bottle of water and tipped her head up so that she could drink.

"Just relax. I'm not going to hurt you. You are my ticket out of this country, so if you just do what I say, you won't suffer any consequences. On the other hand if you fight, things could get very bad for you, I'm afraid."

"I don't know what you've done, but just don't hurt me," Anni said, terrified. Helmut's menacing voice reverberated in her ears. "I don't know anything about what's going on."

In fact, Anni remembered quite a lot. She had a bump on her head which throbbed painfully, but her thoughts were taking on some semblance of normalcy. She figured if she just didn't panic and continued to talk to Helmut Gunn, things would much better for her. That was the only plan she could come up with on short notice.

"They'll be looking for me, you know," she said after a few minutes. She didn't want to enrage Helmut and make him strike her, but she knew he was a brilliant man. Maybe she could talk him into acting reasonably.

"Yes, I'm afraid they are on to me," Helmut said calmly. "It won't do them a lot of good, though. I have the art work stashed where they will never find it." He smirked with satisfaction. Helmut thought he was probably much smarter than any police, and he had absolute confidence in his ability to slip through their fingers.

He gave Anni another drink. "And now, I'm going to leave you for a little while, Anni. I'm sure no one will find you while I'm gone. No one ever comes down here."

He walked past Anni, and she heard his footsteps recede in the distance. She was relieved that he'd gone; at least she could think in peace and maybe come up with a plan. She knew she had one thing in her favor. She had her

Swiss army knife in her back pocket. Helmut hadn't thought to frisk her for anything she could use to escape.

"I love arrogant men," she thought to herself as she felt the knife in her back pocket.

* * * * *

Sam and Ian sat down to think about their strategy. The most important thing was finding Anni. Sam's cell phone rang, and it was Joel Drake.

"We're over at Helmut Gunn's apartment," he said. "We've found enough evidence to link Helmut with the International art theft ring. He left notes on his computer with the storage room he rented on the East side of Madison. He's got some paintings stashed there."

"What about Anni?" Sam said.

"I'm going to post some officers both at Helmut's apartment and at his office at the University. He'll have to come back at some point to pick up his belongings. We'll nab him. Don't worry."

"In the meantime we're going to start a search for Anni," Sam said. "We're going to call in the rest of the band to help look for her. I'm sure they'll come when we call them. And, Joel, we're going to be packing. We've got permits."

There was silence at the other end of the phone while Joel considered what Sam had told him. But he had confidence in her ability to handle herself. She had solved numerous homicides, and Ian was an FBI agent. He didn't want them to exercise undue force, but considering who they were dealing with; he didn't think that would be a problem.

"All right," he said heavily. "It makes sense, but just don't lose your head."

"We've got some ideas on where to look," Sam said. "The biggest thing we have working against us is time. We don't know how desperate this guy is and what he's capable of. I just want to see my cousin safe."

* * * * *

Terry answered the phone when Ian placed the call. Sam sat at her computer making a list of places to search for Anni. Ian quickly explained the situation and asked if Terry could gather the band to come down.

"We've got four bedrooms in this house and a couple of couches, so we think we could put everyone up who wants to come down," Ian said. "I'll cook for everyone."

"Well, that's reason enough to come down," Terry said, remembering a few meals that Ian had cooked for the band. "We'll be there by nightfall. Don't worry, I'll marshall the troops."

"We don't want to put anyone in danger," Ian said. "If things get too dicey, I'll want everyone to pull out. But this is mostly about conducting a search for Anni. We'll probably have you scour some of the parks around the University. It'll be hard work, but at least the weather is still nice."

"We'll do anything you ask," Terry said. "Don't worry, we'll be there as soon as possible."

Chapter 45

Terry and Nicole were as good as their word. They arrived at Sam and Ian's by dinner time, after calling for directions about which exit to take off of the Interstate.

"It's really easy," Sam assured Nicole over the phone when they called. "Just take the Highway 12-18 exit, and take the Park Street exit off of 12-18. Turn right on to Park Street, and turn right on Johnson Street. We live on Johnson about one mile where you turn from Park Street."

Terry and Nicole were a little rattled when they arrived after navigating Madison streets.

"This place is crazy," Nicole complained a little grumpily. "Why do all of the streets go every which way?" Her back was sore from sitting in their van, and of course true to male form Terry didn't want to use a map. So she had acted as navigator and a few little spats had ensued.

Sam laughed and gave Nicole's arm a comforting pat. "That's why they call it 'Mad City.' But, seriously, thanks so much for coming. We won't put you into any sort of dangerous situation. We'll just have you help us search around the University and hit some of the parks. Anni could be anywhere." Her eyes filled with tears, and Nicole put her arms around Sam and gave her a hug.

Terry and Ian stood there helplessly, but both of them were furious. They couldn't comfort the women, but they could bond with each other.

"I'd like to get that guy into an alley for a few minutes and work him over," Terry told Ian.

"He's a worthy adversary, so we have to be careful," Ian told Terry. "This guy is pretty big, and he's extremely cagey. He's part of an International art theft ring, and he's probably murdered two people. He looks like an iron man from Germany. You know, the kind of guy you don't want to meet in a dark alley."

The doorbell rang, and Alex Jones and his fiancée, Helen Jackson, stood at the door. Alex would never forget how Terry and Nicole had jumpstarted his flagging career and life, and he felt that he owed them. He would help out in any emergency. Helen felt the same way, as she was afraid that she had lost Alex permanently.

Alex had a big grin on his face and one arm around Helen. He gave them a salute and "Alex and Helen, reporting for duty." His grin instantly turned into tightened lips. "Is there any news on Anni?"

Ian, who had answered the door, shook his head. "Nothing yet, but we're happy you've arrived. We can definitely use the help."

"How is Sam doing?" Helen said solicitously. She peered inside the door looking for Sam. "I think I'll just go find Sam and see what aid and comfort I can give." Alex gave her a nod, and she slipped past the men to find Sam.

She found Sam sitting on the couch, telephone clutched in her hand. She looked up and gave Helen a smile of welcome. Sam and Helen had become instant friends, both being personalities that were used to solving problems for people, even if the difference was that Sam dealt with criminals and Helen dealt with the sick.

"We're sure glad you're here," Sam said, giving a big sigh. "The shoe is certainly on the other foot. I'm used to chasing the crooks and helping others. Now I need some help myself." She gave Helen an uncertain smile. Sam was feeling more vulnerable than she could ever remember. Having a family member in danger and missing was a painful experience, and she was incensed and determined to track down Helmut Gunn.

Helen gave Sam a searching look as the series of emotions crossed her face. "We're here to help in any way we can. Don't worry, we'll find Anni. You can concentrate on finding that psychopath."

The doorbell rang again, and Jake Ross, the tall, lanky drummer for *Heartthrob* stood in the doorway, brownish-blonde curls framing his imp face. Rick Hunter, *Heartthrob's* bass player, stood beside Jake. Rick's Huck Finn face that was used to erupting in laughter was serious, lips set in an angry, thin line.

"We're here to help search for Anni," Rick said, and then reverting back to his nature he added, "Besides, I hear the Ian Temple restaurant is open. We can't miss the great grub!"

Ian gave both Jake and Rick a masculine hug and patted them both on the back, trying to rein in his emotions. "I'm sure glad to see you. Now the entire rhythm section of *Heartthrob* is here. We can't miss with the two of you around. Thanks for coming, guys."

Terry, ever the natural leader besides being the leader of *Heartthrob* decided to take charge. He could see that Sam and Ian were trying hard to keep themselves together, not entirely successfully.

"Okay, there are eight of us here, and we have three cars, plus the van," Terry prompted. "I think the first order of business is to assign search quadrants and rendezvous." He pulled four Madison maps from his pocket.

Sam raised her eyebrows appreciatively. "You've obviously got your own plan, and that's exactly what we were thinking of. Terry, you're brilliant."

Terry flushed with pleasure. He had wanted to pull Sam out of her funk, and he knew that if someone initiated the plan of action, she would join in. He smiled to himself, pleased that his plan had worked.

"We can split into four groups, Alex and Helen, Jake and Rick, me and Nicole, and Sam and Ian," Terry went on. "Does each group have a cell phone? Are our numbers punched in? Good. What should we do if and when we find Anni?" Terry looked over at Ian for instructions.

"If Anni is alone, grab her if you can," Ian said. "You should probably take water and maybe some food, say a power bar. She'll probably be hungry. A blanket might not be a bad idea...we don't know where she's been. A First Aid kit would be good. Do you feel up to starting right away? We could check the area right around the University and stay in contact with each other. But first we need to eat. We can't help Anni if we're burned out and undernourished."

Ian went to the kitchen to assemble food. He had already prepared trays of cold cuts, various cheeses and breads to make sandwiches. He had bought plenty of bottled water, pop, and some wine, although the wine would be for later. He put out a bowl of grapes, cut up pineapple, mango, and strawberries.

Dinner was a quick, mostly silent affair as everyone prepared for the task ahead. Sam picked at her food, eyes downcast, and her mood cast a pall over the group. Nicole sat next to Sam on one side, and Helen sat on the other. They tried to engage her in periodic conversation by asking questions about anything but Anni.

Sam was acutely aware that she was the center of attention. She was still in shock over what had happened. Never in her wildest dreams had she imagined that Helmut would kidnap Anni, although she had tried to take steps to protect her cousin.

Sam flashed back to images of their childhood, when she had mostly taken the lead. She knew that Anni idolized her, and she also knew that Anni was waiting for her to rescue her. She set her lips in a determined line. She wasn't going to let Helmut Gunn destroy her family.

As they were eating, the first flash of lightning ripped across the sky. Thunder followed to add to the ominous mood of the dinner table.

"An electric storm," Ian said, glancing outside with a scowl. "Why is it always a thunder storm?"

His Indiana Jones comment elicited nervous giggles around the table. There was a moment of silence, and then Jake Ross decided it was time for him and Rick Hunter to lighten the mood.

"Au contraire," he said with a grin. "I seem to remember another mystery that was solved in the midst of a terrible storm. We didn't do so badly with that one." He cocked an eyebrow meaningfully at Rick, giving him the perfect opening.

"Ah yes," Rick took up the thread that was offered. "We're fairly good at debunking the pretenders to the throne. First there was Sheila...und now Helmut. I do believe we're turning into an International band and detective agency. I think the storm provides the perfect backdrop!"

Another crack of lightning accompanied Rick's statements, and suddenly their activities turned into a quest.

Chapter 46

As soon as the sound of Helmut's footsteps receded into the distance and Anni was sure she was alone, she began to work the knife out of her back pocket. Her fingers felt stiff and cramped, but her headache had begun to recede. She knew she'd also put a little pill container with some Advil in her pocket, so she figured she'd be all right.

She managed to push the army knife towards the opening in her pocket. The knife caught on a thread inside of her jeans, and she had to struggle to work it free. Her shoulders ached with the effort and she once again felt nauseous. She stopped for a few minutes to rest. She was beginning to feel chilled and figured that it must be 5:00 or 6:00 p.m. She fell asleep on the cold cement floor, exhausted from her efforts.

*****

It took a trip to the nearby grocery store and another to a Walgreen's to assemble enough supplies to satisfy Sam. She had shaken herself out of her depression and felt better once she began to take action. It beat sitting around and conjuring up images of terrible fates for Anni.

The band divided up into the four groups they had agreed upon and set off in different directions. Sam and Ian had decided to stick to the University as their designated ground zero. Sam didn't know why, but she was certain that Anni was trapped somewhere on campus. They opted to check as many buildings in the immediate area around Helen C. White as they could.

Sam had also called Janey to update her on the latest developments, and Janey had thought about helping with the search with her two daughters. Rhonda and Kirsten were eager to help their mother and were especially excited when they found out they would be helping Sam and Ian.

"Oh, Mommy, it's just like on tv," ten year old Kirsten screamed in delight. "Are we going to be detectives too? How fun!" She clapped her hands together.

"Maybe we'll find Daddy," eight year old Rhonda said in a sad voice. Rhonda had Janey's blond hair and her father's chocolate brown eyes. Kirsten had Janey's cornflower blue eyes. Both had Janey's petite build.

"There would be nothing I'd like more, honey," Janey replied, giving Rhonda a hug. She ruffled Kirsten's hair automatically as she thought about Rob. She still missed him terribly, but she was determined to live for her daughters and to help Sam and Ian in any way she could. They would help with the search, but not tonight in the storm. Janey wasn't about to subject her girls to any danger.

* * * * *

Sam and Ian began the search by walking through the upper three floors of Helen C. White in the tower section of the building. They checked all the bathrooms, and looked in every office. Bruce Wilkins had given them the master key to the building, which opened all but a few doors.

"I don't think that he would hide her in any office but his," Bruce told them. "He wouldn't have the key. We have a fairly stiff system of security around here, and unless he picked a lock, he couldn't get in. He wouldn't be able to get into our conference rooms, because we have security plates on the doors. We've had break-ins before, and the UW Police helped us to analyze and update our security system in the department. It's a fairly structured system."

As they expected, they found nothing. They decided to check the upper and lower parking areas of the building, which were deceptively large.

They walked down six floors using the stairwell and came out at the area known as "Upper Parking." Sam glanced outside at the parking area opening. That opening was one-half block from the lake, and she walked over to the entrance to look at the water and think.

The storm was now raging full force, with heavy pelting rain and lightning which ripped across the sky like an angry fireworks display. The temperature had dropped almost twenty degrees from the relatively sunny day that preceded it, and Sam shivered and zipped up her fall jacket. She had a hooded sweatshirt on underneath the jacket for insulation, and she pulled up the hood around her auburn curls.

Sam was getting wet from rain blown into the entrance way of the upper parking lot, but the rain helped her to stay alert. Her mind was anxiously shifting through scenarios, and she passed her hand over her forehead in exasperation. She stared over at Memorial Union, a stately building which sat just across Park Street, home to "The Terrace," a gorgeous plaza by the Lake which featured trendy musical acts during the summer for students.

She tried to think like Helmut Gunn. What would she do with a hostage? Why had he grabbed Anni? It was almost like he was thumbing his nose at the Department of Philosophy by nabbing their key administrative figure. Sam knew that the department heavily depended on Anni, and she could only imagine the confusion and terror that her kidnapping had caused. Okay, so the guy was after creating an atmosphere of fear. Nothing more than a terrorist, Sam thought glumly to herself.

But on second thought, Sam didn't think that Helmut Gunn was into politics. If that was the case, he would probably kill Anni, and that was unacceptable. He was an art thief, but he was also probably a murderer. Sam wouldn't let herself follow that thought to its logical conclusion. She couldn't. Anni just had to be okay. She shivered as another clap of thunder rolled and turbulent waves reached from their caldron towards the erupting sky.

Sam's cell phone jangled, and she hastily fumbled for the phone, impatiently punching buttons and talking at the same time.

"This is Sam," she said shortly, wondering if someone in the band had found Anni.

"Sam, this is Joel. We're at Helmut Gunn's place, but he hasn't shown yet. However, a brunette did show up and went into his apartment. She was in there for about an hour and came out with a suitcase. She tried to elude us, but we nabbed her. We're questioning her at headquarters now. Do you want to come and be a part of it?"

Sam thought hard. She wanted to question this mystery lady, but was afraid to leave her post. She fought with conflicting emotions for a few moments while Joel waited for her answer. She could smell the clean air, mingled with the algae smell of Lake Mendota as she considered where she would be the most effective.

"No, Joel. I'll let you handle that, and I have full confidence in your ability to pull as much information out of her as you can. Do you know who she is?"

"Her identification shows her name as Catherine Eaton," Joel replied. "We're running her name through every computer system, including Europol. The FBI has her listed, and we're checking other hits. She is probably a member of the art theft ring. She's no doubt Helmut's girlfriend."

"I really think we should keep looking for Anni on this end," Sam told Joel miserably. Her bottom lip trembled, and she took a deep breath to help hold her emotions in check. She didn't want to lose it on the phone with Joel, as she knew he was feeling the same way. She strove for a thought that would lighten the conversation, but her mind had shut down.

There was a silence on the other end of the phone as Joel sorted through the mixed messages he was getting from Sam. He knew that in this situation Anni would want him to act as much the older brother towards Sam as he had acted with Anni. It wasn't so much of a stretch for him. He already felt that he had known Sam for a long time.

"All right, I assume the band is there helping you look. You might want to call the Physical Plant folks…they know the grounds of the University better than anyone."

Sam was suddenly alert. Joel had unwittingly dropped the answer in her lap, and she had an idea of what she had to do next.

"Joel, I've just thought of something. See if you can wring some answers out of Ms. Eaton. She probably knows where Helmut is hiding out. Let me know what you find out. I've got something I have to do on this end."

Joel was astonished at Sam's sudden change of mood. She was all business, and he knew she had thought of something that might break the case. His hand tightened into a fist.

"Good luck, and I'll be in touch," he said.

Chapter 47

Sam grabbed Ian, who had been walking the perimeter of the parking lot looking at the various doors and making notes. They would have to wait until the next morning to contact Physical Plant and ask them to open some of those doors. He settled for knocking, but they didn't hear anything.

Sam pulled on Ian's sleeve and tried to remain calm. "Ian, we've got to go up to Anni's office. She's got a Staff Directory there, and we can contact Steve Wyatt at home, if there is a number for him. I think I know what's going on."

Ian figured when Sam made that statement, she had probably solved the case. He nodded, and they stepped into the entrance to the elevator and punched the button for the fifth floor.

They entered the Philosophy Department and unlocked Anni's door. Bruce had also provided them with the security key to the department, figuring that they would be a safe bet. Sam rifled through Anni's desk and gave a little cry of triumph as she uncovered Anni's staff directory.

"She's got to be in one of the tunnels," she said to Ian. "I wonder if there's one with a room." She dialed Steve Wyatt's number with shaking fingers.

"There's a room in the basement just across the street in Science Hall," Steve told Sam. "It has a window that faces State Street. Call me if you find anything."

* * * * *

Terry and Nicole scoured State Street, walking as far up as the Capitol Square. Madison's capitol building is one of the most beautiful in the country. The Capitol's marble beauty looked menacing with lightning flashing around its empty flower-lined sidewalks. It looked desolate and deserted, with nothing but street lights illuminating the murky darkness.

"It's like looking for a button in a barn," Terry said dejectedly to Nicole as they stood staring at the Capitol. "Let's turn around and try to find Sam and Ian. I feel like we are on a totally wrong track here."

Nicole looked over at Terry sympathetically. She knew how much he thought of Ian. They are family to us, she thought to herself miserably. She also couldn't let herself think of anything but success in the search, but the storm outside had picked up in intensity, and she was soaked to the core of her being.

"I agree. We're not getting anywhere. Maybe we can check more buildings around campus."

They began walking down State Street towards campus. The storm gradually began to abate, so there was no longer thunder and lightning, just a light drizzle. The buildings looked forlorn in the darkness, and as they passed "People's Park," a small enclave used for musicians and exuberant teens, the empty benches and bus shelters took on an eerie hue as storm clouds scuttled out of the area and moonlight returned. Nicole looked up at the fall constellations that emerged after the storm.

*****

Alex Jones and Helen Jackson gave up their search of the West campus. They checked around every building and walked up Regent Street and past the football stadium, home of the famous Wisconsin Badgers. The stadium loomed in the storm like a Roman colossus, imperial in its sheer magnitude. Alex and Helen gaped as they took in the size of the stadium and its sky boxes.

"Wow...that's quite a structure," Helen finally said. "We'll have to come down for a Badger game sometime."

"Maybe sooner than later," Alex agreed, taking in the sight. Alex was a total football maniac and secretly followed the Badgers, although he and Helen now lived in Minnesota.

They slowly made their way back to Helen C. White, which was their designated meeting place. They hadn't found anything, and they felt that they had let Sam and Ian down. They plodded along through the now diminishing rain, not bothering with conversation. Even though the stars now shone in the sky, their thoughts were glum.

"I sure hope Anni will be all right," Helen said softly, finally breaking the silence.

"Me too," Alex answered quietly. "I don't think Sam would ever forgive herself if something bad happened to Anni. She adores her cousin."

* * * * *

Jake Ross performed a song on his leg with his fingers, as he and Rick Hunter, *Heartthrob's* bass player walked up Observatory Drive. Their plan was to walk to Walnut Street and cut over to the Lake path. Jake and Rick had both become complete mystery buffs after the show at the Target Center when Sheila Star had been exposed as the murderess of LeMar Ridley, *Heartthrob's* booking agent.

Jake and Rick were close friends, and when they walked a little too far and discovered the Nielson Stadium Center, they both gave a little cry of delight.

"I'll bet we could play tennis there," Rick said with a smile. "Did you bring your racket?"

"You bet I did," Jake was not to be outdone by Rick. "After we solve this little imbroglio, I challenge you to a match. The loser has to buy the beer." Jake was the eternal optimist and had every confidence that they would soon catch Helmut Gunn and free Anni. Rick gave Jake a fleeting mocking glance, which quickly turned serious.

"You sound pretty sure of yourself," Rick commented, hoping for a moral boost from his friend.

"We can't lose. We've got the best detective team this side of Minneapolis," Jake laughed, patting his shoulder.

They were thinking the Lake path might be unsafe in the rain, but duty overrode their concerns. They picked their way down to where Walnut Street met the Lake path and turned back towards Helen C. White.

"So this is where Rob McIntyre was murdered," Jake said solemnly. The eerie backdrop of the rain gave way to stars appearing overhead through the canopy of trees that grew around the path as the storm blew itself out.

"It's quite beautiful really," Jake said nervously, seeing a sign in the dark that renamed the lake path for Howard Temin, a cell biologist who used to love to run on the lake path. "But I'll be glad when we get back to meet the others." He looked around as if waiting for a ghost to pop out and tear his eyes out.

Rick laughed uncertainly. For once he couldn't think of a pithy statement to lighten the situation. He just wanted the walk to be over.

* * * * *

Helmut didn't return, figuring that he had Anni stashed where no one would ever find her. He planned on releasing her with a call, but not until he was safely out of the country.

He laughed to himself as he snuck past police, who were looking the other way. At least he thought they were. He planned to slip into his apartment and gather his remaining belongings. He already had his suitcase packed. He just needed two minutes, and he would disappear.

"Hold it right there, buddy," his back stiffened and a wave of dread passed through him as he heard words spoken quietly behind him. He was trapped.

Helmut Gunn didn't lose heart. He figured that whoever belonged to that voice was probably not as strong as he was, and a little smirk appeared as he prepared to turn around to face his accuser. When he saw Joel Drake and took in his linebacker frame, the smile froze.

"I've never said this to anyone before, but I've got you, you son of a bitch," Joel Drake said. He then read Helmut Gunn his rights, and then the lights went out as Helmut punched him and ran.

*****

Anni woke up as the temperature dropped low enough to cause her to tremble. She looked around uncertainly, the events of the day washed over her. She then remembered that she had the army knife hidden in her sleeve. She immediately went to work.

It took about a half hour for her to saw through her ropes. She pulled at the ropes frantically, fearful that Gunn would return. She didn't want to speculate what he might have in mind for her future. Finally the ropes gave, and she pulled her hands out. Her shoulders ached from the effort, and she gave herself a few minutes to gently massage the areas that were most painful.

She looked around. She was in a cavernous room, maybe ten feet by twenty feet. There were brick walls, which looked to be at least one hundred years old, maybe from the Civil War period. Anni figured she must be in an ancient building, and the only location she could think of was Science Hall, right across the street from Helen C. White. She turned around, looking for a door. There was a passage on one end and a metal door on the other. She opted for the door.

She pulled at the door, hoping to find a way out of the building. It creaked as it opened, and she stepped into a strange room that was shaped like a half octagonal. There was an opening to the outside, but there were bars blocking her way. There was no way out. She fought an urge to panic, and settled by letting out a curse. She walked over to the prison-like opening and saw Park Street. She was right across the street from Memorial Union. She began yelling.

* * * * *

Terry and Nicole arrived at the plaza at the end of State Street. Their frustration was palpable, and they didn't speak. They crossed over past the old State Historical Society building when they heard Anni's voice nearby.

"What was that?" Nicole jumped and her heart skittered inside of her chest.

"It was a woman's voice," Terry said, as they both began running towards Science Hall.

* * * * *

Rick and Jake were just rounding the corner past the Limnology Building on the lake path when they heard Anni's voice. They practically crashed into Sam and Ian as they ran out of the building.

Alex and Helen had decided to walk down University Avenue and take Park Street over to the Helen C. White building so they wouldn't get lost. They broke into a run when they heard Sam yell "we found her!"

Rick and Jake flagged down Alex and Helen as they came from the opposite direction. Ian met Terry and Nicole as they approached from the mall in front of the Historical Society.

Sam ran over to where Anni was imprisoned. She looked at Science Hall, trying to pinpoint her location. Her eyes finally settled on the front of the building, behind the austere cement stairway leading into the building. There was an opening behind the stairs with bars on the windows. She rushed over and grabbed Anni's hands, which were frozen.

Sam tore off her jacket and passed it through the bars so Anni could put it on. Her teeth were chattering as much from terror as from the cold, and her eyes were wild.

"I can't get you out this way Honey," Sam said desperately. "Is there a way out?"

"I don't want to go back into that room," Anni whimpered. "What if he comes back?" She clutched Sam's hands harder, eyes desperate.

Sam's heart felt like it was twisting in her chest. "Just sit tight. We'll find the way in and get you out. Don't worry. You're safe now."

Ian was right behind Sam, and the rest of the group was huddled on the sidewalk, watching the proceedings. Ian put his jacket on Sam's shoulders and began issuing orders.

"Terry and Alex, come with me. Rick and Jake, stay here and stand guard. Helen, do you have your cell phone? Call Joel Drake. His number is 251-8795. Tell him to get over here with reinforcements. Tell him we've found Anni. Nicole, stay here and take care of Sam."

Nicole rushed over to help Sam. She pulled gloves out of her pocket and handed them through the bars to Anni. She pulled water and a power bar out of her backpack and also pushed them through the bars.

Sam and Anni were still shaken. Anni put the power bar in her pocket, opened the bottle of water and took a long drink. She couldn't stop shaking, but her tears began to subside. She put on the gloves and grabbed for Sam's hand once again.

"Just get me the hell out of here," she said, lips settling into a grim line. "This place is something out of a horror movie."

Ian, Terry, and Alex ran around to the back of the building and crept inside. They ran down the wide stairs to the basement, where a door with the number 50 loomed in front of them.

They gingerly ascended a set of old metal stairs. At the bottom of the stairs stood a gigantic fan that served the steam heat in the red brick building that looked like a boxy government building with castle turrets and dormers. They turned left around the corner and saw the cavernous brick room where Anni had lain. The steel door leading to the barred opening was opening, and Anni gave a little cry when she saw them and ran into Ian's waiting arms.

Anni once again erupted into tears while Ian held her and Terry and Alex stood by helplessly. Ian let her pent her emotions, and then gently whispered to her that it was time to go.

"Get her out of there right away, Ian," Sam called nervously from the outside. "You never know when Helmut is going to show up again."

Terry agreed. While he was confident of his and Alex's ability to take care of themselves, he wasn't looking for a fight. It was time to get Anni out of there, so he unconsciously took the lead and turned toward the exit.

Alex was feeling particularly angry when he saw what Anni had been through. He was just beginning to gain control of himself after a near career ending experience with his own band and having to prove his innocence as a murder suspect. He and his girlfriend, Helen, were just getting their lives back together. He understood pain better than any of them.

The three men and Anni crept towards the stairway with flashlights shining like beacons to lead them through the bowels of Science Hall. They made it to the top of the stairs, out of door number 50 and were ascending the stairs when they heard the voice of Helmut Gunn.

"Hold it right there."

Ian's heart sank, but he wouldn't let go of Anni. He knew that he had his Beretta 9 mm automatic in his back pocket. He gritted his teeth. He just wanted one chance to get at Helmut Gunn. He decided to get Helmut Gunn talking. His training kicked in.

"So, how did you discover this, er...Gothic setting?" He gave Helmut his sweetest smile, hoping to disarm him.

Helmut gave a self-satisfied chuckle. "Oh, it wasn't too difficult. I was cruising around on the Internet one day and had noticed this building. I found some articles someone had written about it. Did you know that the original Science Hall burned down in 1884? It's all masonry and metal, steel beams, that kind of thing. And it's not Gothic, you twit. It's Richardson Romanesque. The foundation is volcanic rock...rhyolite. There used to be a slide that reached from the roof to the ground that served as a fire escape.

It was originally home for the sciences, including anatomy. They used to have a morgue where med students performed autopsies in the north wing. They were still finding pieces of cadavers as late as 1974. Isn't that a hoot?!

Oh, and there are ghost stories about this place. It looks like a castle, don't you think? There are bats and more than one mystery written about this place. I'm sure if ghosts exist, there are some here." Helmut allowed himself a small smirk. He hoped he was scaring the group silly; he could then make his getaway.

"I asked some of the guys from Physical Plant what the basement looked like. They were kind enough to take me down here. It wasn't too difficult to lift a key from one of them. He left it in the lock." Helmut congratulated himself on his own resourcefulness.

"So, what now," Ian asked, hoping to keep him talking. It worked perfectly. Until his partner showed up, Helmut had been alone for several months and enjoyed the discussion. He began to spill his guts in a long, rambling dialogue.

"We've had this art ring for years. It's so simple acting as a visiting professor, you see. No one suspects, especially in the Philosophy departments. I've made enormous amounts of money," Helmut bragged.

"So where are you off to now?" Ian asked, his hand gripping the gun tighter. He just wanted to keep Helmut talking, hoping that he might find an opening or Joel Drake would show up with reinforcements, although Ian halfway hoped he could tear this guy apart with his own hands.

"Well, it was simple, until you and your girlfriend messed things up for me," Helmut said with a smirk. "Now I'll have to figure out how to dispose of all of you."

"Tell me more," Ian egged Helmut on.

"Where should I start? I'm not in a hurry to kill you," Helmut said mockingly.

That's what Ian was counting on. He gave Helmut a wicked smile, held Anni a little tighter with one arm, and let his hand hover over his gun with the other for just a second before letting it drop to his side.

Chapter 48

Sam and Nicole were getting restless. Rick and Jake joined them, and Helen stood off to one side, uncertain as to what she could contribute, but she figured her nursing skills would come in handy when they brought Anni out. Helen glanced at the bars on the front of Science Hall nervously. She couldn't imagine what Anni had been through. She hugged herself as she waited.

Right now Jake Ross felt like he could jump out of his skin. He looked over at Rick for support and maybe a quip. Rick was always good at defusing a situation.

Rick was known as the Huck Finn of the band, usually full of jokes and a carefree attitude. Rick stood uncharacteristically mute. He hoped that Ian and the others had found Anni safely and hadn't run into any difficulties.

Sam pulled out her gun as two squad cars drove up quietly. She put her finger to her lips as Joel Drake pulled his muscular girth out of the squad. Joel in turn turned to Howe, Smith, and a third officer named O'Hara. They had a taser and three additional weapons among them.

"Now where is Anni?" Joel demanded in a whisper.

"Ian, Alex, and Terry went around to the back of the building to find a way in. They've been gone too long for my comfort, and I'm afraid Helmut may have returned," Sam said. "We'd better go check on them."

"We're right behind you. That sonava bitch got away from me once, but I won't make that mistake again," Joel said, as he signaled for his men to fan out around the building. He didn't want to make a lot of noise, so he used various hand motions to let his officers know where he wanted them.

They snuck around to the back of Science Hall. It was immediately obvious what was happening. Helmut and Ian were talking, and Ian had a firm grip on Anni. But Helmut had the gun.

Joel once again signaled, this time to Sam, to back him up. He crept up behind Helmut as he was bragging to Ian, Terry, and Alex, all of whom looked furious. To their credit, they didn't flinch when they saw Joel appear, but continued talking to Helmut.

"Give her to me now," Helmut said, waving his gun around dangerously.

Joel looked around at Sam. She had her Sig Sauer covering his back. He pulled out his own Glock 17 and stuck it in Helmut's back.

"Hold it right there, buddy. You want to be famous? I can help. Now, it's time to get down on the ground and spread 'em, asshole." He then read Helmut Gunn his rights as pulled his arms behind his back and slapped handcuffs on while Helmut cursed.

Sam walked over to where Helmut lay on the ground, arms pulled behind his back. His mouth was pulled back into a snarl, and his eyes were glittering with hate as he looked up at Sam.

"I'll get you for this," he roared.

"And I'm not a cop anymore," Sam said as she gave him a hard kick in the ribs. Helmut crumpled.

"Sam!" Ian said to her, and as she turned he gave her a huge hug.

"Sam, you're a chip off the old block," Joel cried as he roared with laughter. Everyone else clapped.

Chapter 49

It was wedding day, and once again the band gathered in Minneapolis. The ceremony was especially festive, with two brides instead of one.

Patty Boyd and Robert Pierce, and Alex Jones and Helen Jackson were the two radiant couples. Patty and Helen had both decided on Christina Wu dresses. Patty, with her artistic flair, chose a white strapless ball gown with a natural waistline, semi-cathedral trail, and a floor length hemline. Her black shag hair was tweaked into a sweeping and sophisticated hairdo.

The more conservative Helen, after careful thought and many sleepless nights, had chosen an ivory sheath with short cap sleeves, a v-neck covered with Schiffli lace, and a sweep train and angled hemline with more lace. She wore ivory ribbons woven into her brown hair, and the effect was stunning.

A short ceremony ensued with a full church of family, musicians, and friends from Minneapolis, Madison, and Cleveland. Nicole played organ and Terry sang on all songs but one. Alex Jones wrote a song especially for Helen, and stepped up to sing a little shyly. His beautiful tenor voice rang with conviction, and the tender lyrics left many in tears. All too soon it was over, and the crowd trooped over to the Target Center for the reception after the "I do's" were completed and the couples kissed to thunderous applause.

The *Heartthrob* roadies had set up the band equipment to Terry's specifications. They scaled down the usual amount of equipment to set the tone for a wedding reception and also to allow for jamming with other musicians who attended the event, including *Phoenix Bookings* bands. Since Patty and Robert had taken over the booking agency, the area bands had rushed to sign with them, and they could barely keep up with the new traffic.

Once again, *Heartthrob* took to the stage. Both Nicole and Terry were in fine voice, and the band enjoyed playing a "no pressure" gig to a dancing crowd, instead of the more formal concert setting. Alex left his bride to join the band onstage, and he and Terry traded guitar licks on one of their songs. Nicole danced around the stage, singing harmony and clapping her tambourine against her leg when she wasn't playing keyboards.

Sam sat at the table with Patty, Robert's new wife; Jake's wife, Darby; and Rick's wife, Suzanne. Darby looked much like Elizabeth Taylor, with short black curls and violet eyes. She loved to wear violet, and wore a crepe knee-length dress with cap sleeves. Suzanne's auburn hair was long and lustrous, and offset her burgundy v-neck cocktail dress. Darby and Suzanne both worked as secretaries at an insurance company and enjoyed a close friendship, which was a natural offshoot of their husbands' rapport.

Helen Jackson Jones came over to the table and gave Patty's hand a squeeze. Anni, wearing a black cocktail dress that offset her blond hair, also joined them at the table. They listened to the band for several minutes, enraptured with the setting and relishing the harmonic sounds of great music.

Close to the end of the first set they looked at each other, questions to explode from restrained, but curious psyches. Darby took the lead, as she often did, in getting the conversation started.

"Okay, you guys, out with it. What happened down in Madison?"

Anni looked over at Sam, giving her the old "you take the lead," eye signal. Sam took a deep breath and quickly outlined the details of the case, beginning with Rob McIntyre's death. She held the table spellbound with her tale, and they didn't even notice that the band had taken a break until Nicole and the rest of the band joined them.

"I don't understand," Helen commented. "Why did Helmut Gunn have to murder two people?"

Sam glanced over at Helen. "We think that Rob McIntyre saw a picture of one of the pieces of art that Helmut had stolen on his computer. Helmut was sure that Rob was going to report him. The art ring was established enough so that he was afraid of exposure, so he decided to bump Rob off. We think that Marie Cavendish may have seen something. She was too hysterical to talk about it at first, and before Joel's people could get back to her, Helmut had already found her and finished her off. It turns out that she and Helmut had dated, and she caught a glimpse of him running from the scene. She called out for him to help her with Rob, but he was the murderer. So she sealed her fate."

"It was such a waste," Anni said. "Helmut was a brilliant person, but his greed just got the best of him. He also dealt drugs. What a jerk. And to think he tossed Janey's home, not to mention the mess he made of my apartment, and me, for a few excruciating hours."

"He was trying to scare Janey into calling off the investigation," Sam said. "When that didn't work, he thought he'd kidnap Anni to give himself some leverage." She shook her head, still furious.

Nicole had quietly walked up to the table just as Sam paused. She had already heard the story and just wanted everyone to have a good time at the reception. She casually changed the subject.

"So, ladies, how is the band sounding?" Nicole asked innocently, knowing that they had been talking about the case. Her strategy worked.

"You guys are just incredible," Anni said, eyes shining. "I just wish I had a dancing partner. You don't happen to know any eligible bachelors, do you? I'm sure I could keep some stunning man entertained with our latest exploits." Anni had just finished putting her apartment back together two days before the wedding and had recovered from her scrapes and bruises.

Just then Anni caught sight of a blond haired man who was just about her age. He looked strangely similar to Ian, and she shook her head as she did a double take. All eyes turned to investigate the source of Anni's sudden distraction. They saw a man who looked hauntingly similar to Ian, but with curly blond hair cut in a shorter style.

"Hey, James," Ian called. "Come on over here. I have someone I'd like you to meet."

"Who is that guy?" Anni breathed. "Do you know him? He's absolutely gorgeous!"

"Oh, he's my cousin," Ian said cheerfully. "Didn't I ever tell you about him?" He chuckled as Anni punched him in the arm.

James walked up to the table with a twinkle in his eye. His eyes swept over the ladies in a appraising but non-threatening manner. They rested on Anni, and the two locked eyes.

Ian smiled in amusement. "Anni Cassidy, I'd like to introduce you to my cousin, James Temple. We're related on my father's side. His father and mine are twin brothers, and James got the blond hair. I take after my mother as a redhead."

"Hmmm," Anni said, and James slipped into a seat beside her. Suddenly the night was that much more dazzling. She and James immediately began a conversation, leaving the others in the dust.

"What do you do?" Anni asked James to open the dialogue, feeling a little self conscious.

"Oh, I'm a cop," James grinned down at her. "Would you care for the next dance?"

Anni gave Ian a bewildered look that silently asked him if James was someone she should avoid.

Ian gave her a reassuring glance and replied to her silent query.

"It's all right, Anni. It runs in the family. We protect our loved ones. He's all right; I'll vouch for him."

They walked out to the dance floor and started a slow dance to a Steve Perry song that the band played on a boom box while they were on break. They didn't say much, just enjoyed the feeling of each other as if they had been together before. The music stopped and they returned to the table.

Joel Drake and his wife, Keisha, appeared and chairs scrapped along the floor to make room for them at the crowded table. Joel was wearing a huge grin, along with a grey pin-stripped suit and pink shirt. He wore a brand new tie with darker shades of pink and grey to complete his ensemble. His chocolate brown eyes twinkled.

Keisha was a small, petite African-American woman with shoulder length hair pulled back from her face. She wore a burgundy cocktail dress that was made of silk and moved with the contours of her muscular body. She was breathtaking, and she and Joel greeted the group warmly.

"I see you've recovered from your nasty experience," Joel said to Anni, as he and Keisha gave her a hug. Introductions were made all around, and the conversation naturally turned to the arrest of Helmut Gunn.

"We think we've got the entire ring," Joel said proudly. "We've recovered the pieces they stole from the Art Institute, and they should be returned in a couple of weeks. We've tied Professor Gunn to several art robberies, and he has been giving us information about his partners in exchange for a more lenient sentence. His female partner was quite a canary." Joel laughed at his last statement. "They were both connected to a small drug ring out of Minneapolis."

"Helmut Gunn will be lucky to escape with a prison sentence. Wisconsin doesn't have the death penalty, and most of the European cities we've tied his crimes to don't, but there are other elements we have no control over. It seems that he took hefty advances from certain, how do I say it, criminal elements. They might not be so nonchalant about the loss of their money."

"You saved my life, Joel," Anni said softly. She turned to the rest of the group. "How can I ever thank all of you? You worked together to save my hide." Tears appeared in her eyes, and she fought to control the sudden rush of emotions that seemed to suddenly burst like a crumbling dam from her psyche.

"Oh, I'm sure you'll think of a way to heal," Sam said gently. She looked over at James, who seemed confused by the conversation. "Maybe you can start by having a drink with this guy and relating your adventure?"

"Indeed," Ian winked at his cousin. "She has quite a tale to tell."

* * * * *

Later that evening Sam and Ian crawled into bed; their bones aching and heads reeling from the partying and the release of tension. Cleo and Quincy fought for position on the bed, and they each took a kitty to scratch. Each cat had a distinctive purr, and in tandem they sounded a little like a small electric mixer.

"It's finally over," Sam observed after a few minutes of comfortable silence. "Anni is safe. The murderer is caught. Rob McIntyre will be avenged."

"I missed seeing Janey and the girls at the reception," Ian commented.

"Oh, they decided to stay home and celebrate with each other," Sam replied. "I hope they will be all right.

Janey dropped off a check for $45,000 today while you were in the shower. She said she will be eternally grateful and will keep in touch."

Ian whistled. "That should keep us solvent for a few months. How about a cruise during spring break? Maybe we could talk some people in the band into coming." He paused for a few seconds, took a deep breath, and forced his mouth to form the words.

"Of course, we could get married, and then go on a trip to the Caribbean?" He snapped open a ring case that he had been hiding under the covers. "That is, if you'll still have me."

Sam took the ring case, opened it, and saw a gleaming diamond ring that Ian had had designed.

"This is a down payment on the rest of our lives. What do you say? I told you that I was committed to you forever."

"Yes!" Sam squealed, hugging him. "But we're going to have to wait until I can take a break from Law School. This is going to take some planning, but I love the idea of a cruise…with the sun; the open sea; little drinks with umbrellas in them; lots of food; and no dirtballs around."

She threw her arms around Ian's neck. "Maybe we could have the band play for our wedding? Oh, this will be so much fun. But you have to promise me one thing."

Ian cocked an eyebrow at her. "And what is that?"

"No murders on this trip," Sam laughed.

"Indeed," Ian muttered as he bent to kiss her.

THE END

Printed in the United States
115199LV00003B/194/A